Jimmy Dabble

Jimmy Dabble

Written and illustrated by
Frans Vischer

DUTTON CHILDREN'S BOOKS • NEW YORK

Thanks to Wayne Carlisi, Jeff Johnson, Mike Kunkel, Edmund Fong, Dusty Horner, Nancy Newhouse Porter, Kristie Hubbard, Sarah Ketchersid, and Fran Coleman. Thanks also to Mam and Pap.

———

CIP Data is available.

Published in the United States by Dutton Children's Books,
a division of Penguin Putnam Books for Young Readers
345 Hudson Street, New York, New York 10014
www.penguinputnam.com

Designed by Alyssa Morris
Printed in the USA
First Edition
ISBN 0-525-46671-1
1 3 5 7 9 10 8 6 4 2

This book is dedicated to my wife, Jennifer.
Thanks for your support, wisdom, and love.

Contents

Jimmy Dabble

1

The Dabbles

There once was a beautiful valley covered by acres of rolling farmland and fertile pastures. One end of the valley was bordered by a deep, dark wood, and in the center of the valley, on top of a slight hill, stood a small yellow farmhouse owned by Hank and Maggie Dabble. They were not wealthy people, but this day they felt as rich as anyone in the county—for Mrs. Dabble had just given birth to a little baby boy. They named him Jimmy.

Jimmy arrived like a ray of sunlight in the drab lives of his parents. Mr. and Mrs. Dabble's financial difficulties had given them a very serious view of life, and this had caused them to think of nothing but the routine of their chores in tending to their little farm.

Mr. Dabble was a kindhearted, skinny man with a long nose and a shock of curly brown hair. He never ate very much, because he firmly believed in being frugal with all things. An unlit pipe always dangled from his lips, since Mr. Dabble could not afford to buy tobacco.

Mrs. Dabble was a worrywart. She worried about the weather and whether the chickens laid enough eggs and especially about money. Years of worrying left tiny worry lines fixed on her forehead. Even when she had nothing to worry about, she found *that* cause for worry.

Jimmy's parents were people of few words, but Jimmy changed all that. When he was only three months old, he spoke his first word. "Cuckoo!" blurted Jimmy, copying the bird who sprang from the clock on the kitchen wall. Naturally, his parents were delighted. By the time he was five months old, Jimmy was speaking entire sentences and talking nonstop. "How come the sun always wakes up when we do?" he asked his father.

"Because it's time for work," replied Mr. Dabble.

"But what if the sun is too tired to get up?"

"That's no excuse for not working, son," said Mr. Dabble, before he hurried off to the barn.

"Does a yellow flower ever wish it was pink?" Jimmy asked his mother.

"No, Jimmy," answered Mrs. Dabble as she washed the kitchen windows. "We can't change what we are."

"Do leaves get hurt when they fall down?"

"No, son."

"Do they cry when you step on them?"

"Leaves don't have feelings, Jimmy," replied Mrs. Dabble with a deep sigh. Answering Jimmy's constant questions kept his parents very busy, and they became quite frustrated when Jimmy disrupted their daily chores.

Then Jimmy learned to crawl, and one day, when he was about nine months old, he climbed out of his crib. Mrs. Dabble found him in the fireplace, covered in soot. She gave Jimmy a bath and put him back in his crib—but as soon as she turned around, he climbed out again. Mr. Dabble found him by the barn, playing with a pitchfork. He held Jimmy tightly and said, "You must stay in your crib where it's safe, Jimmy." Pipe in hand, he pointed frantically to the edge of the valley. "Those woods down yonder are dangerous!"

"There are ghosts that live in the trees and wolves that eat little children!" Mrs. Dabble added for good measure.

Mr. and Mrs. Dabble hoped that this was the end of little Jimmy's exploits, and things could get back to normal. But Jimmy was a curious child, and the next day, while his mother washed the windows upstairs and his father milked the cow, he climbed out of his crib and crawled down the hill and into the woods.

It wasn't long before Mrs. Dabble discovered that Jimmy had gotten out of the crib again. She searched the house and the yard. Together with her husband, she searched every inch of the farm, but Jimmy was nowhere to be found. With help from some neighbors, they combed the hillside and nearby farms. Fearing the worst, they entered the dark woods. Armed with clubs and rifles and flashlights, they searched for hours, keeping in close contact with each other so no one would be lost.

The woods were eerily quiet, but for the shouts for Jimmy. Thick gnarly roots covered the ground, and intertwining tree branches blocked out the sun. All day long they searched, but Jimmy couldn't be found. As the sun went down, they headed back to notify the police. To their great surprise, however, Mr. and Mrs. Dabble spotted Jimmy by the little gate, sound asleep, wrapped in a colorful woolen blanket. Overjoyed, they took him in their arms and hugged and kissed him endlessly. Wiping away tears of joy, Jimmy's parents thanked their neighbors, and tucked Jimmy into bed.

The next morning Jimmy hopped onto his parents' bed and blurted, "Mommy! Daddy! I met a strange creature in the woods! He was big and hairy, and he jumped up and down really high!"

Mr. and Mrs. Dabble were horrified. "Don't tell fibs, Jimmy!" said Mrs. Dabble.

"Especially after breaking our rules!" said Mr. Dabble.

Jimmy's parents forbade Jimmy to talk about the woods and set him back in his crib, which they kept in his room. But Jimmy was bored there. Except for a picture of a boy with red hair, standing in a field with his arms out-stretched, the walls were bare. So Jimmy climbed out of the crib again and again. His parents spent the entire day chasing after him, while the dirty dishes sat unwashed and the corn went unpicked. At last, out of sheer desperation, Mr. Dabble built new rails for the crib that were too high for Jimmy to climb over and escape.

Jimmy tried and tried, but the rails were simply too high, and he finally gave up. He sat down and began telling his parents about a hairy creature in the woods. But they absolutely didn't want to hear it and demanded he keep quiet. So Jimmy stopped talking.

2

A Discovery

Two years passed. One warm spring morning, Mr. and Mrs. Dabble woke up, as usual, just before the crack of dawn without the aid of an alarm clock. Jimmy heard his parents tiptoe down the stairs to start their chores. After breakfast, Mrs. Dabble put Jimmy in his crib, where he played quietly with his toys from the thrift shop: an old sheep and a cow made of wood, which were dented and had paint chipped off. The cow had three wheels attached underneath—the fourth one was missing.

Through the bars of his crib, Jimmy watched his mother

dust the porcelain figurines in the living room cabinet. The figurines were her most treasured possessions, and she handled each one with great care. After she dusted the girl holding the blue umbrella, she polished the little boy in patched overalls clutching a fishing pole. The boy selling newspapers was next. Jimmy had his parents' routine memorized and amused himself by pretending to control them. When he clapped his hands and pointed to the kitchen floor, his mother promptly began mopping it.

"A day of hard labor gives the soul something to savor!" said Mrs. Dabble, quoting from a framed embroidered picture hanging on the kitchen wall. She washed and dried the dishes, hanging the serving utensils neatly in a row above the sink, from smallest to largest. Jimmy knew exactly where everything went. His mother lined the coffee mugs on the counter with the handles to one side, always in the same order. Mr. Dabble's first, followed by her own, then Jimmy's little cup.

At precisely three o'clock the kettle whistled. Jimmy's mother took the once-used tea bags from their dish on the windowsill and hung them in the teapot. Since this was the first clear day in months, Mr. and Mrs. Dabble decided to take their tea outside, and they moved Jimmy's crib out to the porch. Jimmy had gotten so used to being in his crib all day long, he didn't want to leave it. Each time Mr. and Mrs. Dabble tried to take him out, he cried. But Jimmy loved being outside, because then he could see the farm animals.

A grand total of three dozen sheep, three chickens, a pig, and a cow lived on the Dabble farm. The old cow was the first to take an interest in Jimmy. The bell around her neck rang a gentle melody when she walked, and Jimmy hummed along as the cow came closer. Her large belly seemed all out of proportion to her thin legs. Jimmy couldn't decide if she was white with black spots or black with white spots, since there seemed to be even amounts of both. She peeked into the crib, smiling sweetly at Jimmy. He smiled back and held up his toy cow, proudly pointing out the way he had fastened a button from his shirt in place of the missing wheel.

At three-fifteen Jimmy's parents resumed their work. By the time Mrs. Dabble had rinsed the dishes, the chickens—who had followed the cow—were perched on Jimmy's crib rails. The red one hopped inside the crib, and the way she strutted around, cocking her head this way and that, Jimmy knew she was inspecting him. "He looks perfectly normal!" she squawked.

"He's too quiet, Janet," said the black one. "Kids should be noisy!"

"I rarely agree with Bridget's cockeyed opinions," exclaimed the white one boldly, "but I'm actually with her on this one. He's not normal."

"Cockeyed opinions?!" countered the black chicken. "Pardon me, Joy, but what is *that* supposed to mean?"

"I happen to recall last fall when we were discussing your diet, and you had the ridiculous idea of . . ."

The cow cut in. "Ladies, ladies. Please—act civilized!"

But they kept on squawking like gossiping grannies at a tea party. Jimmy found them most entertaining, and his joyful giggles soon brought the sheep over. Jimmy thought they were the most polite creatures on the farm. Unlike the chickens, the sheep were always in complete agreement.

"Make way, make way!" a tiny voice shouted from among

the sheep. The pig emerged from the forest of wool. He was really just a piglet, barely big enough to look into Jimmy's crib. He had a short snout and long floppy ears. "I want to see! I want to see!" he demanded in a pip-squeak voice.

"Hi, Al," shouted Janet, "we're checking out the kid!"

Al grunted, straining for a better view. The bickering squawks of the chickens, the cow's scolding *mooo*'s, and the soothing harmony of the sheep made for a wonderful racket, and Jimmy smiled with joy.

"Land sakes, Hank!" Mrs. Dabble said, rushing over, "look at Jimmy and those animals!"

Mr. Dabble came by for a better look and said, "Leave him be, Maggie. Thank the good Lord he's found some company."

The next day Jimmy's mother set him outside again, and it wasn't long before the animals visited him again. The black and white chickens perched on the rail of the crib, squawking loudly when the old cow came marching toward them. "Is it true?" she asked with great concern, "she didn't lay an egg again this morning?"

"Yes, Suzy," squawked the white chicken.

"That's the third day in a row," added the black chicken.

"The poor thing," said the cow. "She must be worried sick."

"I heard the Farmer this morning talking with his wife," said the white chicken. "Janet's headed for the stew pot if she doesn't start laying soon."

They grimaced at the thought. "What does that mean?" squeaked the pig.

"You're too young to understand, dear," said Suzy.

"No I'm not!"

"Should we talk to her about it?" asked a sheep.

"No!" replied the white chicken sharply. "You know how sensitive Janet is about that."

Jimmy listened intently to the conversation, concerned by Janet's dilemma. "Quiet, everyone!" said the cow. "Here she comes!"

The red chicken emerged from the chicken coop, her head hanging down.

"*Ssh!!* She's headed our way!" gasped a sheep.

"No one say a word!"

"Just act natural," a sheep whispered under her breath. "So," she began far too loudly, "think that cloud up there looks like Aunt May, or what?!"

Janet joined the group. She hopped onto the railing and into the crib, next to Jimmy. The animals stood frozen. Dozens of eyes darted nervously around for what seemed like a very long time.

"I'm sorry you couldn't lay an egg today, Janet," said Jimmy calmly.

The animals gasped, shocked as much by what Jimmy had said as by the fact he'd understood what they'd been saying. Janet eyed Jimmy with suspicion. "How do you know my name, young man?" she squawked.

"Oh, I know all your names," replied Jimmy matter-of-factly. He pointed to the two chickens on the crib rail, who stared back wide-eyed, and said, "Your names are Joy and Bridget. And you are Suzy," Jimmy said to the cow, who nervously backed away a few steps.

"And I'm?" the pig prodded.

"Al!" Jimmy cut in.

"Yes!" squealed the pig, jumping up and down excitedly.

Quickly recovering from her shock, Suzy uttered sweetly, "Hello, Jimmy. It's nice to meet you."

"Pleasure to meet you, Jimmy," squawked Joy, the white chicken. "I'm a leghorn."

"Well, *I'm* a Plymouth Rock," said Bridget, the black one with little white stripes, proudly puffing out her chest, "a most respectable breed."

Joy turned to Bridget with disgust. "*My* family has a long tradition of first-class stature, I'll have you know!"

"Just ignore their squabbling, Jimmy," said Janet as she

stepped onto Jimmy's lap. "Happens all the time. I'm a Rhode Island Red myself. Not proud of it, not ashamed of it. It's just how I was born."

"It's nice to meet you all," said Jimmy. Then he rattled off the names of the sheep, all thirty-six of them, without making a single mistake.

Janet suddenly let out a loud squawk. Wide-eyed and smiling, she stood up and blurted, "Well, for Pete's sake, I laid an egg!"

She stepped aside and, indeed, there on Jimmy's lap lay a shiny, brown egg. "Well done, Janet!" exclaimed Jimmy.

The animals congratulated Janet and began talking excitedly. Bridget and Joy hopped into the crib and hugged her. "Listen, everyone!" exclaimed Jimmy. "We've got to put this egg in Janet's nest so my father will know it's hers!"

"But how?" asked one of the sheep. "We don't have *fingers*!"

"*I* do! *I* can carry it!" Jimmy said excitedly.

"But you can't get out of this crib, remember?" blurted Bridget.

"I can help there," said Suzy. She pushed one of her horns between two bars of the crib rail and said, "Hop on, Jimmy!"

Suzy's horns weren't very big, but there was just enough space between them for Jimmy to stand. Suzy raised her head, lifting Jimmy to the top of the railing. Holding the egg in one hand, he climbed over the railing onto Suzy's back and slid to the ground without dropping it.

3

Farm Chores

Jimmy had never held an egg before. It felt warm in his hands, and he ran in small strides so he wouldn't trip, for he knew what a precious thing it was. Al scrambled around Jimmy's feet, trying to be helpful. "Make way, make way!" he shouted, but he only made things more difficult for Jimmy. Janet ran alongside them, watching anxiously. "Careful! It's very fragile," she squawked.

"Out of his way, everyone!" barked Bridget, directing traffic.

"Give him space!" shouted Joy, as Jimmy entered the

coop. "If he drops that egg, Janet will . . ." She wisely decided to hold her tongue.

Janet pointed to her nest, and Jimmy gently set the egg down in it. Janet plopped down with a heavy sigh of relief, and Jimmy sat down beside her. "What a nice house," he said.

"Well," said Bridget dryly, squatting down on her nest, "it's a bit drafty, but it's home."

Just then Mr. Dabble appeared. He bent down and peered into the coop with a stunned expression. Scratching his head in disbelief, he shouted, "He's here, Maggie! In the coop!"

Jimmy pointed proudly to Janet's egg. "Well, I'll be darned," said Mr. Dabble. He grabbed the egg just as Mrs. Dabble arrived and handed it to her. "She's still layin' after all," he said.

For a moment Mrs. Dabble smiled, but the worry lines quickly returned to her forehead. "How did you get out of your crib, Jimmy?"

Jimmy pointed to Suzy, who quickly looked away. Mrs. Dabble gave the cow a puzzled look. Then she continued, "You gave us a mighty fright, son."

"He's nearly four, Maggie," said Mr. Dabble. "I reckon he's safe in the coop."

"I reckon," Mrs. Dabble said at last. "But stay by the house, Jimmy. Those woods down yonder give me a terrible fright!"

Jimmy nodded obediently. When his parents were a safe distance away, the chickens let out a sigh of relief. "Thanks, everybody!" said Janet happily. "Especially you, Jimmy! You saved my tail feathers!"

"You're very welcome, Janet," said Jimmy proudly, gently stroking her neck.

"What an eventful day this has been," said Suzy, sidling up against the chicken coop.

To Jimmy she looked bigger than usual now that he was seeing her from ground level. Her large belly hung right in front of his face. Jimmy peered underneath, blurting, "Can I squeeze milk from your balloons?"

"You mean my *udder*," Suzy said with a chuckle. She shook her hips a bit and said, "Well, I'm nearly full. Go on, then."

Jimmy scrambled out of the chicken coop to fetch the milking bucket and stool from the barn, as he'd seen his father do. He sat down on the stool and took a firm hold of Suzy's udder.

"Goodness me!" Suzy squealed. "Not so tight!"

"Oh, sorry," said Jimmy, quickly letting go.

21

"Now squeeze gently as you pull," said Suzy cautiously, "and aim at the bucket." Jimmy carefully followed Suzy's instructions and, indeed, a thin stream of milk squirted out.

"That's it," said Suzy, smiling proudly, "now relax one hand while you squeeze with the other."

It didn't take Jimmy long to get the hang of it. As milk squirted into the bucket in a steady rhythm, Al and the sheep gathered around to watch. Janet, Bridget, and Joy hopped onto Suzy's back and nestled together. Suzy began relating the sad story of one of her relatives, who lived on a nearby farm and was allergic to milk. "Even the *smell* of it made her sneeze so wildly that it knocked the Farmer to the ground!" she said with great dramatics.

When Suzy's milk ran out, Jimmy started carrying the bucket to the kitchen. On the way, his father happened by. "Here, son!" he said, quickly taking hold of the bucket before any of the precious milk could be spilled. "Where on earth did that come from?!"

Jimmy lowered his head, as if he'd been caught doing something naughty. "There," he said, pointing to Suzy's udder.

"I know *that!*" said Mr. Dabble harshly. But then he had a change of heart. "Thanks, son," he said, patting Jimmy on the head, "but milking time isn't till four." As his father carried the bucket to the house, Jimmy dashed back into the chicken coop with a satisfied smile on his face.

The next morning, without a word, Jimmy went to the kitchen pantry, fetched the egg basket, and headed for the chicken coop. "Good morning, ladies!" he said cheerfully.

"A good morning it is indeed, Jimmy!" they replied.

Jimmy collected their eggs, set them on the kitchen counter, and dashed out again. Mrs. Dabble stood over the trash can, scraping the previous day's coffee grinds off the paper filter so it could be reused. Mr. Dabble nudged her, motioning toward the kitchen window. Together they stared in silence as Jimmy grabbed the bucket with the chicken feed and started feeding the chickens.

When he was finished, Jimmy milked the cow. Then he swept the barn and replaced the hay so the place was neat and clean for Suzy. After tidying up the sheep's pen and feeding Al, he gathered the sheep together for roll call. Mrs. Dabble rushed toward Jimmy and hugged him tightly. Mr. Dabble rubbed his hair and said, "You do us proud, son."

Jimmy took on all the chores that involved the animals, and he spent nearly all his time with them. "I don't know what he sees in those animals," said Mr. Dabble, and Mrs. Dabble shrugged in response. But they were happy that Jimmy had become a part of their daily routine. Like clockwork, each day passed no differently than the one that preceded it. The days quickly became weeks, which became months, and then years.

4

Summer Vacation

As he walked along the dirt road that ran past his house, Jimmy hummed a happy tune. His schoolbooks, tied together with a belt, swung casually from side to side. School had let out early, because it was the last day of the year. Jimmy had a long summer ahead of him, away from all the kids who teased him for being so quiet and made fun of his secondhand clothes, which were faded and covered with patches. He felt much more comfortable on the farm, where he could talk with the animals or otherwise be left alone.

Jimmy had grown taller and lankier. In two months he would turn nine, and although his shoulders were still narrow, his hands were big and strong. Off to his left were the dark woods. To his right, up the hill, was his parents' farm. Jimmy hopped the fence and entered the meadow, and the sheep raced to greet him. "Ready, go!" he shouted, and they trooped up the hill. As usual, Jimmy finished dead last, with the exception of Rowland, a kindly sheep who always let Jimmy finish ahead of him.

Jimmy guided the sheep into their pen as he greeted Suzy and the chickens. Al leapt from the mud bath he was enjoying and approached Jimmy like a faithful dog. He'd grown into a humongous hog, and his tiny squeaks had developed into a golden tenor voice. "How ya doin', Jimmy?" he said.

"Just fine, Al!" Jimmy petted him and entered the kitchen, just in time to see the cuckoo clock strike twelve. Jimmy loved noon, because that's when the little bird said *cuckoo* more than any other time of the day.

Mrs. Dabble stood by the counter preparing lunch, which was always the same: two pieces of lightly buttered wheat bread, with a thin slice of cheese in between. And, as always, at the twelfth *cuckoo* Mr. Dabble stepped inside. He struggled to untie his bootlaces, which had five knots in them, while Mrs. Dabble set out the food.

They sat at the table, waiting, as Mr. Dabble took his seat and began eating. Only then did Jimmy and Mrs. Dabble reach for their food. "I know you got your heart set on a fishin' trip this summer, son," Mr. Dabble said in between bites of his sandwich, "but we just can't afford it this year."

"Corn crop was bad, wool prices are down," added Mrs. Dabble.

Jimmy nodded. He didn't expect to be going anywhere this summer, since they never went anywhere during the summer—or at any other time of year, for that matter. Not another word was spoken as they ate their lunch, until Mrs. Dabble spotted the mailman through the window. "Mail's here," she said.

Mr. Dabble got up and opened the screen door, which was so full of patches you could barely see through it. "You got another card from your mother, Hank," said the mailman. "Sounds like her travelin' days are over."

"Thanks, Sam," replied Mr. Dabble. He closed the door and read the card, as Jimmy and his mother looked on with equal curiosity. "Better prepare a room, Maggie," said Mr. Dabble. "She arrives in two days."

"Well," said Mrs. Dabble, slightly taken aback, "it's been a long time."

"Before Jimmy was born," agreed Mr. Dabble. "Reckon she's got some stories to tell."

"That's another mouth to feed," mumbled Mrs. Dabble, as worry lines spread across her forehead.

Mr. Dabble's mother had lived in Holland since her husband had died many years ago. She'd spent the last few years traveling around the world. The only contact Mr. and Mrs. Dabble had had with her was an occasional postcard from the exotic places she visited. "You're finally going to meet your grandma, son," said Mr. Dabble.

"You'll get on fine with her, Jimmy," added Mrs. Dabble.

Jimmy nodded and finished his lunch. Then he dashed into the chicken coop to tell the animals the news. Al lounged comfortably beside the coop, since he'd grown too big to fit inside. "It'll be nice to see a new face around here," he said.

But the chickens reacted more energetically. "I've got to make myself presentable!" Bridget squawked as she scurried back and forth.

"I must get my claws done!" Joy remarked excitedly.

"Look at my feathers," Bridget lamented, flapping her wings nervously. "They're completely ruffled!"

"You sound like a couple of old hens," squawked Janet.

Jimmy hardly heard them. He saw his mother clearing out the little room down the hall while his father built a ramp by the front door. Mr. Dabble was pounding nails with his hammer when he whacked his thumb. *"Ouwwww!"* he yelped. He threw the hammer down in disgust, mumbling something Jimmy couldn't hear.

Jimmy had to laugh a little. Then Janet hopped on his lap. Gesturing toward the nearly completed ramp, she said, "Your grandmother must be something really special!"

"I guess so," Jimmy replied softly.

5

Oma

Jimmy gazed out the window at the rolling green fields as he bounced up and down in his seat. The shock absorbers on his father's old truck should have been replaced long ago, but Mr. Dabble was determined to get a few more miles out of them. Occasionally the truck hit a pothole, which sent Jimmy bouncing almost to the truck's roof. But he was so excited to be on a trip—even if it was only to the train station—that he barely noticed.

The station lay at the edge of town. The town was small, and so was the train station. A tiny brick building stood adjacent to a covered platform. Jimmy's father parked the truck. He checked the schedule—a quick read, since only two trains stopped by each day.

Before long the train whistle sounded in the distance. The platform began to shake under Jimmy's feet. The brakes made a tremendous racket, a deafening high-pitched sound of steel scraping against steel. With a hiss, the train came to a halt. The doors opened and several people got off, but none of them looked like a grandma to Jimmy. A man in a uniform appeared in the doorway and slid a long wooden board onto the platform, making a ramp. He went back into the train, and suddenly there arose a loud commotion.

"Keep your hands off, young man! I do this myself!" barked a croaky voice.

Mr. Dabble rushed forward. Just then an old woman in a wheelchair appeared in the doorway and rolled down the ramp. "Make room!" she shouted. Mr. Dabble jumped aside as she zoomed by, bouncing onto the platform. She veered around in a wide circle, heading straight toward Jimmy, and screeched to a halt just in the nick of time. "Sorry, boy!" the woman blurted. "I think my brakes need replacink!"

Jimmy's father stepped beside the wheelchair and gave

the woman a pat on the shoulder. "Hello, Mama. It's good to see you," he said.

"Henry!" the woman replied in a boisterous voice. To Jimmy's shock, she flung her arms around his father and gave him a hefty hug. "How are you?" she bellowed. "Vell, I can see, you are skinny. You don't eat enough! I haf a talk vit your Maggie."

"I'm fine, Mother," said Mr. Dabble, rolling his eyes uncomfortably.

Jimmy hid behind his father, staring at her with wide open eyes. She looked nothing like his mom or dad. She was big and round, barely fitting into her wheelchair, and she spoke in a strange accent. Her large eyes bulged out as she spoke, and her mouth was so wide that it seemed too big for her face. A bright yellow hat with sunflowers on it sat on her head. A few gray hairs hung loosely from beneath the brim. Large carved wooden earrings dangled freely. One was rectangular in shape, the other round. Three bracelets on each arm jangled together. She wore a long loose dress with a flower design that had more colors in one pattern than Jimmy had ever seen in his whole life. Jimmy's gaze caught her eyes. "Who is this young man hidink behind you, Henry?"

"Oh, this is your grandson, Jimmy," said Mr. Dabble, yanking Jimmy in front him.

"You have a son?!" the old woman cackled. "Heaven's alive, this is *vonderful* news! Climb up here, boy, and gif me a bik hug!"

Jimmy felt awkward and backed away. He shyly put his hand out for a handshake, but his grandmother's thick arms reached forward and whisked him onto her lap. Her powerful hug nearly squeezed the breath out of him. "You made me a grandmama, Jimmy!" she blurted out. "You call me Oma!"

Jimmy made no reply. He was stuck like a pig packed in a crowded pen. "What's the matter," Oma asked, "the cat has your tongue?"

Jimmy still made no reply. "What's that?" said Oma, playfully holding a hand to her ear. "My hearink is not good."

"I didn't say anything!" blurted Jimmy.

"So you *do* talk! I'm so glad for that!" Oma laughed uproariously. Jimmy felt his grandmother's grip loosen, and he leaped down from her lap.

"It's gettin' on supper time. Let's head home," said Mr. Dabble.

"C'mon, Jimmy, ve race!" Oma blurted.

She rolled her wheelchair away and disappeared in a

cloud of dust. Jimmy just looked at his father. "It's all right, son," said Mr. Dabble as he picked up Oma's luggage. "Let's go."

Jimmy watched his father help the old lady into the truck. The man from the ticket office helped Mr. Dabble carry the rest of Oma's stuff, and soon the flatbed was filled with boxes and crates. Jimmy climbed in back and found a place to sit on a trunk right beside Oma's wheelchair. As the truck drove off, Jimmy peered inside through the window and studied his grandmother. She was talking up a storm, but Jimmy couldn't hear her over the noise of the engine. Doesn't she ever stop talking? he wondered.

The answer, Jimmy quickly learned, was *no*. At afternoon tea, Oma launched into a lengthy description of her most recent travels in a remote part of Asia. But with her first sip of tea she stopped cold. Contorting her face, she blurted, "You call *this* tea?!"

"Tea bags do just fine a third time, Mother," replied Mr. Dabble calmly.

"Bah!" said Oma. "Vat is the joy in life if you cannot haf a decent cup of tea? I buy new tea tomorrow!"

After tea, Jimmy dashed into the coop to tell the chickens all about his strange grandmother, and he stayed there until the supper bell rang.

"Haf you ever seen a llama, Jimmy?" asked Oma, without waiting for Mr. Dabble to start eating. She took a mouthful of mashed potatoes. Jimmy shook his head. He'd never heard of llamas before. "I saw many ven I visited South America. You know vat llamas do ven you stand too close by?" Oma didn't wait for Jimmy's reply. "Spit! They can get you from ten feet avay! Right in the face. Nearly got me once or tvice!"

Jimmy's father grunted in reply. Mrs. Dabble said, "You don't say?"

"Of course I *do* say!" exclaimed Oma, as she piled more corn on her plate. "I just told you so!" Then she carried on.

"And boy, it vas hot there along the Amazon! Made your armpits greasy like a fryink pan!"

Throughout the meal Oma spoke nonstop with great enthusiasm. Her arms were in constant motion, and with each gesture her bracelets clanged loudly. Jimmy watched with bewilderment as she knocked over her milk glass and Mrs. Dabble jumped to catch it before too much milk spilled.

After the longest meal Jimmy had ever had, Oma sank into Mr. Dabble's favorite chair and announced, "I'm tired!" Then she promptly dozed off. Jimmy sat perfectly still. His parents exchanged glances, savoring the silence. The cuckoo clock ticked quietly on the wall, and the crickets chirped merrily outside. Then Oma began to snore.

"I'll put her to bed," said Mr. Dabble.

"I'll clear the table," said Mrs. Dabble.

Jimmy quietly went up the stairs and disappeared into his room.

6

An Intrusion

The following morning, Jimmy and his parents did their usual chores while Oma slept. When she woke up, Mr. Dabble moved her stuff into the tiny room, which quickly became crammed so full that soon only a narrow path to the bed remained.

As Oma finished unpacking, Jimmy peered inside. The floor was now covered with stacks of books that nearly reached the ceiling. Records of all kinds of music filled the shelves and night table. Not a square inch of open space was left—the room overflowed with stuff. The room was a complete mess, but Oma seemed right at home. She placed a sculpture of a dancing cow on the nightstand and said, "Come in and haf a look!"

But instead Jimmy ran straight out of the house to the chicken coop. After lunch, he busied himself with the animals. He was cleaning Suzy's hooves (a little luxury she adored) when Oma rolled her chair down the ramp. "Vant a ride on my veelchair, Jimmy?" She popped a wheelie and formed some figure eights, which made the animals scatter to and fro. When she stopped, Jimmy was nowhere in sight.

When the coast was clear, Jimmy reappeared and then climbed on some hay in the chicken coop to share a story with his friends. Jimmy loved telling stories to the animals. Janet, he felt, had an especially good ear for stories. "Once there was a bear named Theodore who lived in the woods," Jimmy began. "Theodore had a terrible problem. He always sneezed at the absolute worst possible moments, like when he was hunting for food. The rabbits and squirrels always ran away when he sneezed, and he never caught anything. So Theodore was a very skinny bear."

Suddenly the *snap!* of a breaking twig startled them all.

They looked up to see Oma nearby in her wheelchair. The animals quickly scattered in all directions. Jimmy remained frozen to the spot.

"I'm sorry," said Oma in what for her was a soft tone. "I didn't mean to interrupt your story."

Jimmy didn't reply, so Oma rolled her wheelchair to the edge of the coop and peered at him through the chicken wire. "I couldn't hear all of it, but I think that vas a humdingink story, Jimmy," she said. "You sure know how to entertain your friends."

Jimmy looked away, and Oma turned her wheelchair around. "I'd like to hear vun of your stories some time," she said quietly.

Jimmy watched with suspicion as Oma slowly rolled away. When she was gone from sight, Janet uttered, "Boy, did she give me a fright."

"Yeah, me too," Bridget added, shaking her red comb.

"That thing she rides around in could crush my toes," said Joy.

"I think she should be avoided at all times!" Bridget stated flatly.

Returning to the coop and overhearing them, Suzy said, "Well, I don't think she's bad at all."

"Yeah. She's just a little different is all," said Al.

The sheep agreed with Al and Suzy, but to maintain the peace, they quickly made it clear they didn't disagree with the chickens, either. Despite their good intentions, a big argument broke out, which gave Jimmy a good laugh.

THAT NIGHT AT SUPPER Jimmy quietly ate his corn cakes. Oma spoke nonstop, although, to Jimmy's great surprise, she said nothing about his talking with the animals.

The next morning, as Jimmy cleaned the barn, the sheep played tag nearby. When he heard one of them cry out, Jimmy raced outside, but Oma was already there. A lamb named Dorothy lay on the ground beside her wheelchair. Jimmy quickly hid behind the barn and watched as Oma lifted Dorothy onto her lap.

"Poor dear, you tvisted your ankle," said Oma as she tied a handkerchief around Dorothy's leg. "But I haf you jumpink again in no time!" Oma softly stroked Dorothy's wool as the lamb lay contentedly in her lap. She placed her carefully on a bale of hay and left.

Jimmy approached Dorothy. "Are you all right?" he asked.

"Fine and dandy!" replied the sheep. "That grandmother of yours is a peach!"

Jimmy inspected the handkerchief and said softly, "That's good."

All at once a glorious sound filled the air. Jimmy moved toward it and discovered that it came from Oma's room. The music was loud and powerful and startling to him. His parents never listened to music on the radio in order to save electricity. Jimmy went inside. The door to Oma's room was slightly open, the music getting even louder as he edged closer. He stood by the door and listened.

Suddenly a thin book slid out at Jimmy's feet from under the door. He looked at the book for a moment. Then he picked it up and ran off to the chicken coop.

7

A New Friend

With the chickens peering over his shoulder, as Al and Suzy and some sheep looked on through the chicken wire, Jimmy examined the book. It was filled with colorful pictures of a brave knight on the back of a big white horse and a ferocious fire-breathing dragon who lived in an enchanted forest, where he guarded a beautiful princess.

"Wow . . ." Jimmy sighed. He'd never seen a book like this. He leafed through it, stopping at the pages with pictures. It looked much more interesting than the books at school, and the only reading materials Jimmy's parents had were tractor manuals and seed catalogs.

"That little guy is going to fight the big dragon?" Joy asked dubiously.

"And save the beautiful princess?" Bridget added.

"And marry her for the happy ending?" Janet piped in. "Well, start reading! I can't stand the suspense!"

It began to rain, and the animals snuggled close together to keep warm. Jimmy started reading. "In a dark and gloomy forest, in a land far away, there lived a dragon so fierce that no one dared even to set foot in the woods. . . ."

The rain poured for two hours as Jimmy read without stopping even for a moment—so enthralling was Oma's book. "I think we've been wrong about your grandmother," Joy remarked abruptly.

"I still think she's nuts," said Janet, "but I like her!"

"Me too," added Bridget, and the sheep all nodded in agreement.

"She's a very sweet lady," Suzy exclaimed boldly as Al hummed a little I-told-you-so tune.

"You're right," said Jimmy, hanging his head. "I haven't been very nice to her." He turned to Suzy. "What should I do?"

"You should thank her for the book," said Suzy.

Summoning his courage, Jimmy went straight into the house and knocked on Oma's door.

"Who is there?"

"Jimmy," mumbled Jimmy.

"Vell, hello, Jimmy!" bellowed Oma. "You're just the person I must see!"

"I am?"

"Yes! But I can't see you if you are hidink behind the door!"

Jimmy stepped inside the room but stayed near the door. He looked at all the books stacked around the room. Even the school library didn't have as many books. Jimmy spotted *Robin Hood* and *The Three Musketeers*. Oma sat behind Mrs. Dabble's sewing machine, surrounded by rolls of colorful fabric. "Vell, come in—I do not bite!"

"Thanks for the book," Jimmy stammered shyly, his eyes fixed on the floor.

"Vat? I cannot hear you!"

"I really like your book," said Jimmy, a little louder this time. "Thank you, Oma."

"*That* I am glad to hear!" said Oma. "Did your animal friends like it too?"

"Yes . . ." Jimmy hesitated, then added, "They can't read. I read it to them."

"I can tell that you are good friends vit them!" said Oma, smiling broadly. "Does that friendly cow haf a name?"

"Yes, it's Suzy!" exclaimed Jimmy, "and Janet and Joy and Bridget are the chickens' names! They crack me up, they argue all the time." Jimmy climbed onto the bed— the only place there was to sit—and scooted close to Oma. He rattled off all the sheeps' names, and after darting a quick glance at Oma, said quietly, "Mom and Dad don't know their names. They think they're just dumb animals."

"Vell, aren't they missink out on a party!" said Oma. "Have a lolly, Jimmy!" She laughed and handed Jimmy a large yellow lollipop with a purple swirl in the middle. Jimmy's eyes widened. The closest he'd ever been to candy was peering through a store window! He took a long lick and felt the sweetness spread across his tongue.

"Thank you, Oma!"

"Velcome to you!" said Oma, resuming her sewing. "I am goink to call you Pollyvog. Is that all right?"

"You mean, like a tadpole?" Jimmy wondered.

"That's right! A frog that has not yet lost his tail." As the sewing machine purred, Jimmy watched Oma expertly handling the material, swiftly moving it around as the needle pulled the thread up and down. "You remind me of myself ven I vas young, Jimmy. Of course, that vas a lonk time ago."

It was difficult for Jimmy to imagine Oma as a little girl. And yet her eyes were those of a child, so alive they seemed to dance. "I grew up on a farm just like this vun, Pollyvog! I used to run back and forth across the fields, playink vit the sheep and hidink in the tulip fields."

She stopped sewing and said with a mischievous smile, "My favorite place of all vas in the voods nearby the farm."

Jimmy grew quiet. "I'm not supposed to talk about the woods," he said. Baffled, Oma stared at him. "Mom and Dad don't want me to."

"But the voods are the most vonderful place in the whole vorld! I used to go explorink there for hours. You never knew vat you vould find!"

"My folks say it's a scary place."

"Vell, it sure vasn't ven I was young!"

Jimmy wanted to change the subject. "What are you making?" he asked.

Oma turned the sewing machine off and held up a pair of brightly colored overalls with shiny brass buttons. "Try these on, Pollyvog!" she said.

Jimmy was speechless. He'd never seen pants like these. They were bright red with blue and green stripes that con-

nected a pattern of small yellow squares. "I bought the material in Africa," said Oma.

Jimmy put the overalls on. They fit perfectly. "Thank you, Oma."

Oma smiled. "I overheard you tellink the chickens that the kids at school tease you about your clothes. Maybe now they vill be *jealous* of you!" Jimmy beamed with pride, and Oma continued, "I made the pockets extra big so you can collect thinks." Lifting the lid of a battered old box, she removed a knotted handkerchief and opened it up. Inside was a round object, which she pressed into Jimmy's hand.

"What's this?" he asked.

"A compass."

"What's a compass?"

"It is an instrument that helps you find your vay."

Jimmy held the compass close to his face. The metallic edge was rusty and scratched, and the glass was faded. But the dial and letters underneath were clearly visible. Jimmy turned it in his hand and noticed that the dial always pointed in the same direction.

"Do you see, it alvays points to the north? That is how you keep from gettink lost. I used to play vit that compass in the voods. It's old now, but it still vorks!" With a wink she whispered, "Better keep it in your pocket."

The kitchen clock struck six times. "It's supper time, Oma," said Jimmy as he marched proudly into the kitchen.

The sight of Jimmy in his new overalls nearly gave his parents heart attacks.

"What on earth are you wearing?" shrieked Mrs. Dabble.

"And what's that you're licking?" barked Mr. Dabble.

"Oma made new overalls for me, and she gave me a lollipop!" Jimmy replied happily.

Mr. and Mrs. Dabble didn't approve of the lolly. As they sat down to eat, they were quick to point out to Oma that, in their opinion, candy was a waste of money and only led to trips to the dentist, and dentist visits were very expensive. "The clothes we give you are just fine," Mrs. Dabble said curtly.

"But they look funny," Jimmy protested. "No one else at school has patches on their clothes!"

"Eat your peas," said Mr. Dabble.

For the rest of the meal, nobody said much. Oma was quieter than she'd ever been, and after supper she excused herself and went into her room. Jimmy helped his mother clear the dishes. Then he went up to his bedroom with Oma's book under his arm.

8

Knights and Dragons and Goblins

The next morning the sun shone warm and bright. As the sheep grazed peacefully in the meadow below, Jimmy sat in the shade of an oak tree with Al by his side, engrossed in Oma's book. Besides the dragon, there were also trolls and goblins in the enchanted forest who hunted fairies at night. The sheep frolicked in the tall grass, calling Jimmy to join them, but he was so intrigued by the book he barely heard.

Eventually, when Jimmy did look up, he spotted some-

thing darting into the woods. He sat bolt upright, staring intently, but nothing appeared from the trees. Al was sound asleep. Jimmy felt an urge to investigate—but just then the lunch bell sounded. So he woke Al, gathered the sheep, and headed home.

That afternoon Jimmy couldn't stop thinking about the woods.

"Are you feeling okay?" asked Janet. "You look like you've got your head in the clouds."

"I just have some things on my mind," Jimmy replied.

When Oma gave him a ride on her wheelchair, he didn't tell her either. Oma played some opera records for Jimmy and explained the plots of the stories, which helped take his mind off dragons and goblins. But as soon as he climbed into bed that night, Jimmy's thoughts returned to the woods.

The next several days, while he and Al watched over the sheep in the meadow, Jimmy eagerly gazed down at the woods, searching for any signs of life. His curiosity grew, but each time the lunch bell rang, he dutifully returned to the farm.

Every chance he could, Jimmy read a few pages of Oma's book. But he was often interrupted. "Jimmy, you forgot to clean the barn," said his mother. "Put that book down and get to work!"

"But Ma, I'm on the last chapter!"

"Jimmy!"

"Yes, Ma." And while he swept the barn, he told the animals about what he had just read. "The dragon has Princess Penelope up in his castle tower, and he's about to eat her, and Prince Gallant comes to rescue her, but he's stuck in the quicksand that surrounds the dragon's castle! His horse, Trottalot, is trying to save him, but he's running out of time!" Jimmy quickly hung the tools on the barn wall—in their proper order, from shortest to longest—and rushed into the chicken coop to savor the final chapter.

But before he'd even opened the book, Jimmy's father appeared. "Did you do the toothpicks yet, son?" he asked.

"Oops!" Jimmy scurried into the house, but by the time he'd finished washing all the used toothpicks, it was supper time. "Mom, can we wait ten minutes with supper? I've just *got* to know if Prince Gallant will kill the dragon and save the princess!"

"We always have supper at six, son," said Mrs. Dabble as she dished up the potatoes.

"You've been neglecting your chores, Jimmy." Mr. Dabble held up a box of toothpicks. "These things ain't cheap, son."

"You're spending too much time reading that book," added Mrs. Dabble.

"Oh, but it's such a neat book!" Jimmy protested. He explained about the trolls and the fairies who lived in the enchanted forest, and how they helped Prince Gallant find the dragon's castle. But this only gave Mr. and Mrs. Dabble further cause for worry. They turned to Oma with stern expressions.

"I don't believe this book is right for young 'uns," said Mrs. Dabble.

"Maggie, it is just a storybook," protested Oma.

"It's interfering with his chores, Mother," said Mr. Dabble. "Give me the book, son." Jimmy did as he was told and stomped out of the kitchen. Oma looked on sadly, but said nothing. Jimmy kicked open the screen door and ran to the chicken coop. As the chickens gathered around him, he told them why he wouldn't be reading them the final chapter of the story. He'd never been this angry at his parents before.

"What's so bad about Oma's book?" asked Janet.

"Beats me," replied Jimmy. He tore up some straw and threw it in the air. The straw fluttered down on Bridget's head, but Jimmy was too angry to notice.

While Bridget cleaned herself off, Al tried to lighten Jimmy's mood. "Well, I sure like your pants!" he blurted cheerfully.

"Yes," added Joy supportively, "they're so colorful!"

"And real pockets too!" said Bridget. "The old socks your mom used for pockets were ingenious, but not very classy!"

But Jimmy only frowned. He was still pouting the next morning as he headed toward the meadow with the sheep. Al trudged faithfully behind him. Mr. Dabble had given Jimmy his newest tractor catalog, and Mrs. Dabble had put jam on his toast, which normally happened only on Sundays. Oma offered Jimmy a ride on her wheelchair, but nothing could cheer him up, and Jimmy left the house without a word.

Brooding, he sat down in his usual spot under the oak tree. Dark clouds loomed overhead, and down below, the woods looked mysterious and inviting. Al lay down quietly, seeing no need to speak. Jimmy played with Oma's compass. Oddly, the arrow pointed straight at the woods.

Just then, Jimmy saw something moving among the trees. In an instant it was gone. He sat up and stared, his heart pounding so hard he thought it would explode. The sheep were grazing peacefully and hadn't seen a thing. Neither had Al. In a flash, Jimmy raced down the hill as fast as he could.

9

The Dark Woods

He was out of breath when he reached the edge of the woods, but Jimmy charged on without looking back. The excitement of being somewhere he shouldn't be simply overwhelmed him. The trees stretched out above him like spiders, their branches sprouting in all directions. Some had long, prickly thorns. Gnarly roots poked up from the ground and reached as high as Jimmy's head. One tree with a twisting stem begged to be climbed, and in no time Jimmy was perched on one of its branches, looking down on his world. The woods went on as far as he could see, so Jimmy climbed down and continued to explore.

An underground tunnel intrigued Jimmy, and he bravely crawled inside. But it was dim and dark, and he quickly turned back. As Jimmy ventured deeper and deeper into the woods, the thick overgrowth gradually blocked out the sky. Thoughts ran through his mind of trolls and goblins lurking behind the trees, but other than some squirrels and the occasional butterfly, he saw no signs of life. It felt as though a hundred eyes were staring at him, and Jimmy wished he had a flashlight. As he passed underneath a tree root, a sheet of thick moss dragged across his face, making him jump. "There's nothing to be scared of," Jimmy told himself. But the lure of the forbidden, and the sense of looming adventure, sent a tingle through his body.

Vague memories flashed through his mind, as if he'd seen this before, but Jimmy dismissed them as dreams. Leaves rustled overhead, and plants brushed up against his legs. He thought about his parents' warnings of wolves in the woods. There was just enough filtered light to make out a spiderweb as big as a tabletop! A screeching owl whooshed low over Jimmy's head, and that did it. As shivers shot

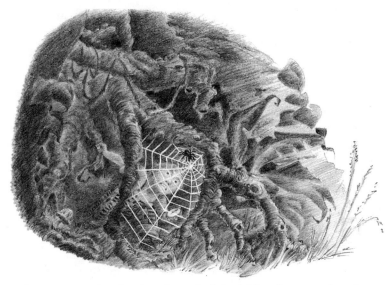

through Jimmy's body, he decided he'd had enough adventure for one day.

He turned back, and using the compass to guide him, Jimmy came to a clearing. A large oak tree with sprawling branches stood in the center. Draped in sunlight it was a welcoming sight, but Jimmy kept going. For several minutes he walked, moving quickly through the foliage, climbing over tree roots and ducking to avoid spiderwebs, when he came upon the same clearing again. "What's wrong with this thing!" he snapped at the compass.

Jimmy studied the shadow underneath the oak tree. The sun was directly overhead and therefore no help in giving direction. "Darn, it's nearly lunchtime!" Jimmy muttered. "I've got to get home!" Although he was losing faith in the compass, Jimmy knew it was his only hope. Reluctantly he pressed on. Carefully following the movements of the dial, Jimmy turned every which way it did, and it appeared he was making some headway until he arrived at the clearing for the third time.

"Oh no!" Jimmy uttered in despair. Angry, he flung the compass at the oak tree, shouting, "Stupid thing!" The compass bounced off the trunk and landed in the grass. Tired and disheartened, Jimmy plopped down at the foot of the tree. "Why did I listen to Oma?" he grumbled. "I'm in big trouble now!"

While Jimmy contemplated his fate, a *swish!* sound startled him. He looked up. No one was there, but the compass was gone. Leaves rustled wildly above his head, and he crouched down, frantically peering among the branches for any signs of life. He backed away and was about to run when he was suddenly whisked up into the branches. In the next instant, Jimmy found himself high up in the treetop beside a very odd-looking creature.

"*Aaaaaaaaaaa!*" Jimmy screamed and kicked and jerked with all his might, but he could not break free from the

creature's long, gnarly tail firmly wrapped around his waist. Then he saw the ground some forty feet below and quickly averted his eyes to keep from getting dizzy.

The creature had a pig's nose and a mouth the shape of a hippo's. He was about five feet tall, with legs like those of an elephant, but covered in a fur as soft as a bunny rabbit's. One of his tiny hands clutched the compass, while the other held a bright red, pumpkin-like fruit.

"Let me go! Put me down!!" Unfazed by Jimmy's screams, the creature casually sucked a purple-colored goo that looked like Jell-O from the fruit. In between slurps, he hummed a jolly tune, while turning the compass in his hand and tilting his head to study it from all angles.

Realizing that shouting had no effect, Jimmy uttered in a softer tone, "Excuse me. Hello?" But the creature didn't react at all. "That's *my* compass, you know," said Jimmy, tired of being ignored. "I believe you took it from me!" The creature spit out some seeds and licked his lips with a long, blue tongue and went on playing with the compass.

"Oh never mind!" said Jimmy impatiently. "You can have it. Stupid thing doesn't work anyway!" The creature continued humming merrily, and Jimmy folded his arms in a huff. "Fine! Ignore me! See if I care!!"

Undeterred, the creature took a few more bites, made a

satisfied grunt, and uttered in a slow, deliberate drawl, "Most yummy fruit come from vine that grow freely."

Jimmy stared at him, completely baffled, not sure if what the creature had said was even directed at him. "What . . . ?" he uttered in confusion. The creature turned to Jimmy and smiled, but he said nothing more. "I have to get back for lunch," said Jimmy, gesturing toward his belly. "Hungry? Eat?"

The creature offered the fruit to Jimmy, exclaiming, "Goozers have taste of a most yummy-yummy way." His voice was deep and gravelly.

Jimmy was about to decline the offer when he realized it might be wiser to accept, just to avoid upsetting his captor. "Thanks!" he said, pretending to be delighted. With the utmost of self-control, Jimmy dipped his finger in the purple goo and reluctantly licked it. To his great surprise, it tasted pretty good. "Hmmm," he said, "that's not bad!"

The creature nodded, but quickly cautioned, "Watch for seeds!" and sprayed a few of them toward the ground. His tail loosened from Jimmy's waist, and Jimmy clutched the branch with his arms and legs to keep from falling.

"What do you call that?" Jimmy asked, partially out of curiosity, but mainly to be polite.

"Goozers," replied the creature. He broke the fruit in two

and tossed Jimmy a half, which he managed to catch one-handed, while carefully maintaining his balance.

"Hmmmmm, it smells like that black licorice at the candy store," Jimmy said with a smile. "I never knew it tasted like this." The creature chuckled, sounding like Santa Claus's *ho ho ho*, only in slow motion. Jimmy took a big slurp, then asked, "What are you, anyway?"

"Beebo."

"Beebo? What's that?"

"Me."

The creature had a funny way of speaking. His answers sounded more like questions to Jimmy. "No, I mean, what kind of animal are you?" continued Jimmy. "I've never seen anything like you."

The creature shrugged his shoulders, and uttered, "Beebo is Beebo!"

Jimmy muttered, "I see," but he really didn't. Then he coughed and a seed shot from his mouth, hitting the creature's forehead. "Oh!" Jimmy blurted, "I'm really sorry!" But the creature burst into a jolly fit of laughter. Then he took aim and spit several seeds smack onto Jimmy's nose.

"Hey!" exclaimed Jimmy. "I said I was sorry—"

But before he'd finished the sentence, the creature hit him again, this time on the chin. "Ouch!!" Jimmy shot a

few seeds at the creature, who ducked to avoid them, and
hit Jimmy three times in the chest. "Ouww!!" exclaimed
Jimmy. The creature was enjoying himself immensely, and
when Jimmy attempted another shot, he jumped off the
branch with the ease of a monkey, laughing as he disappeared among the leaves and branches.

Jimmy looked down, and with a shudder he turned away.
"Hey, don't leave me up here!!" he shouted. From below he
heard a *boooooiiiing!* sound, and a moment later the creature appeared, right in front of Jimmy. He shot two seeds
onto Jimmy's forehead and dropped back out of sight.

"That was a dirty trick!" There was another *boooiing!* and Jimmy prepared himself with a mouthful of goo. But the creature came up from behind and shot him in the fanny. "Woooawww!!" Jimmy nearly lost his balance. He dropped his fruit as he clutched the branch tightly. Below he saw the creature bounce on his tail, as if it were a pogo stick, and zoom back toward him.

Jimmy crouched down and was pelted with seeds, and as the creature dropped back down, Jimmy decided he'd had enough. "Hey, get me down!! If I don't get home soon, my trousers are fried!"

"You ask with niceness?" the creature said as he flew past.

"You gotta be kidding," grumbled Jimmy to himself. But then the creature dropped back down, shaking his finger at Jimmy.

"Not kidding!" he said.

"*Please* get me down?!" Jimmy shouted after him.

Boiiiiing! "Now speak with smile?"

Jimmy forced a smile and huffed, "Pleeeeeeese get me down?!"

The creature landed on the ground with a *thud* and remained there, hands at his sides, looking up at Jimmy. "Oh, come on!" Jimmy shouted, "I said *please* and I even *smiled*!

You *promised!*" But before he could complain anymore, the tree started shaking so violently that Jimmy lost his grip and fell down. A blur of branches and leaves zipped by, but he stopped abruptly several inches from the ground, hanging by his feet, which Beebo held with his tail.

Jimmy's stomach sank into his throat as Beebo lifted him, so their noses nearly touched, and calmly uttered, "I bring you home."

Jimmy wanted to tell Beebo that he didn't know where home was, but he was too nauseated to speak. Suddenly they were off, zipping though the woods at incredible speeds, and within moments Jimmy stood at the front door of his house. He grabbed the door handle to steady himself, feeling dazed. Jimmy turned around to thank Beebo, but he was nowhere in sight.

"What's the matter, son?" Mr. Dabble shouted from inside. "You look like you've seen a ghost!"

"Uh, nothing," Jimmy uttered as he stumbled past the door, and he didn't say another word during lunch.

10

Another Visit

Jimmy told no one, not even the animals, about his strange adventure. That night, images of a baby being carried by a creature in the woods flashed through Jimmy's mind, and he awoke feeling quite confused. Many questions swirled around in his head. Who was that creature? Where did he come from? As odd as it was, there was also something familiar about him. Had he dreamt the whole thing? Jimmy *had* to find out, and he determined to visit the woods again.

Jimmy finished his morning chores in record time, kept

conversation with the animals brief, wolfed down his breakfast, and rushed out the door. Jimmy quickly guided the sheep into the meadow and left Al in charge. Then he bolted down the hill. As he entered the woods, Jimmy realized that he didn't have his compass. I must've left it with Beebo! he said to himself. Now I'll never find him again!

He continued walking, determined to try anyway, when something fell and landed right by his feet. It was the compass. Startled, Jimmy looked up. Right above him, casually lounging on a branch, was Beebo. He smiled and chuckled a low, slow laugh.

"Thank you." Jimmy put the compass in his pocket. "You scared me half to death!" But he was happy to see Beebo again. Beebo yanked Jimmy up with his tail and plopped the boy down beside him. "I came *this* close to getting in trouble yesterday!" Jimmy said teasingly, holding his thumb and forefinger one inch apart.

But Beebo wasn't fooled. "Beebo very helpful!" he said, nodding proudly.

"If I'd been late, my parents would've been so angry—" continued Jimmy.

"But you were not late."

"Only because I stopped that silly seed-spitting fight!"

"Because you lost . . ." said Beebo, casually glancing the other way.

"All right," said Jimmy, seeing that he wasn't going to win this verbal duel either. "Forget that. Let's talk about something else." Beebo agreed, and they had a pleasant discussion about things they liked (like wrinkled skin from taking long baths) and disliked (like sneezing with your mouth full). Beebo disliked forgetting to do things he liked to do, and he liked making snowball blueberry snowcones, and playing tag with the fish in the pond.

When it was time to go, Jimmy quickly said good-bye while he had the chance and then found himself alone by the gate of their farm. A little cloud of dust was all that Beebo left behind. Jimmy couldn't wait to tell the animals about Beebo. He rushed into the yard and nearly bowled into Janet. Joy, Bridget, and Suzy were right behind her. "Woaw! Slow down, big boy!" said Janet, straightening her comb. "What's the rush?"

"Did you see him?" asked Jimmy, panting with excitement.

"See who?" asked Suzy.

"Beebo."

"Who is Beebo?" they asked.

Jimmy was about to reply, when his mother, who was hanging laundry on the line to dry, said, "Don't forget the tools in the barn, Jimmy."

"I'll tell you later," whispered Jimmy, and he ran off. Janet and Suzy watched him with curious eyes, and Jimmy shouted back, "I promise!"

"Don't make promises you can't keep, son."

"I was talking to the animals, Mom!"

Mrs. Dabble set the clothespin back in the basket. With worry lines forming on her forehead, she watched Jimmy disappear into the barn. Then she shook her head and returned to her work.

Jimmy washed and hung the barn tools in the usual order, collected discarded cornstalks to be used for wrapping paper, fetched the previous day's newspaper from the neighbors, and sorted the clean straw from the dirty straw in the chicken coop. Then he gathered the animals and told them all about Beebo.

Jimmy was bouncing with energy, but the reaction he got was anything but energetic. The animals sat still, staring with expressions of disbelief as Jimmy described Beebo. "But what *kind* of animal is he?" they kept asking him. Even Al was a bit dubious.

"He's just a Beebo!" said Jimmy. Exasperated, he threw

his hands in the air. But the animals were not convinced and spoke skeptically among themselves. Frustrated, Jimmy left the coop. He was aching to be believed. He went inside and found Oma in her room, knitting a seat warmer for her wheelchair. "Oma. I have to tell you something," Jimmy said. He climbed up on the bed beside her wheelchair and described how he got lost in the woods, even *with* Oma's compass. Oma listened attentively. Then Jimmy mentioned Beebo.

"That's vonderful, Pollyvog!" she bellowed excitedly. The more Jimmy described Beebo, the more enthused Oma became. "I'm so happy you had this adventure!" Oma said. "The voods are a magical place! Vas I right?"

"You're right, Oma!" replied Jimmy, happy to at last have found someone who shared his excitement. When he went outside, the animals were still hotly discussing the issue of Beebo. Jimmy started doing his chores, and the animals followed him around like ducklings after their mother. No one said a thing for some time. Finally, as Jimmy filled Al's trough, Janet blurted, "So, are we ever going to meet this Beebo character?"

"I don't know," said Jimmy. "I'll invite him next time I see him, if you like." That started another debate among the animals, and Jimmy went into the barn shaking his head.

The next morning, Jimmy cheerfully led the sheep toward the gate, intending to visit Beebo again, when his father called him from the roof of the barn, which had leaked since the last storm. "Son, I need a hand up here!"

"But I have to take the sheep to the meadow," protested Jimmy.

"You can keep an eye on 'em from up here!" shouted Mr. Dabble. "Let's go!"

And for several hours Jimmy was stuck handing nails to his father. By then it was lunchtime. Afterward, Mrs. Dabble wanted Jimmy to help her in the kitchen with the dishes, then she pointed to a giant stack of potatoes that needed peeling. Jimmy knew he would not be visiting Beebo that day.

11

Time Flies When You're Having Too Much Fun

For several days thereafter, Jimmy was stuck on the farm. Each time he tried to sneak away, his mother had a chore for him, or his father needed him for something. But just when he was beginning to think he'd never see Beebo again, he got his chance. While his parents were busy weeding the cornfield behind the house, Jimmy snuck out the door. He bumped straight into Oma, who winked and handed him some cookies. "For you to share vit Beebo!"

"Thanks, Oma!" said Jimmy. Then he raced down the

hill and into the woods, and before he could even shout his friend's name, Jimmy was scooped up into a tree. "Hi, Beebo!"

"Beebo most pleased to see you back!" He snickered happily.

They sat down on a branch, and Jimmy handed Beebo a cookie. "My grandmother made these. Chocolate oatmeal with chocolate sprinkles and chocolate chips mixed in," he said proudly. "She really likes chocolate!"

As they munched away, Jimmy told Beebo all about Oma. "Oma bake most yummy way, must be good grandma?" Beebo said, licking his chops.

"I agree in a most serious way!" said Jimmy.

Then Beebo said, "Now I show you," and he whisked Jimmy high into the air. Leaping from tree to tree, he used his tail like a monkey to swing among the branches. Jimmy gripped Beebo's fur tightly, and narrowed his eyes to slits as the wind hit his face. His hair lapped wildly, and the bottom of his shirt crept up to his neckline. Jimmy's grin was as wide as a sunflower.

Suddenly they plopped down on the ground, and Jimmy found himself in a place he could hardly have imagined. They landed right beside a small stream. Bright orange, green, and blue rocks lined the bottom. Gold and silver fish swam around. A small waterfall nearby created soothing waves that rippled across the water, making the giant lily pads sway gently. One lily pad the size of a tractor tire held a quartet of bullfrogs who were croaking in rhythm.

Flowers of many colors and shapes were everywhere, the likes of which Jimmy had never seen. Bell-shaped flowers dripped yellow dew onto some roses below, mixing with their colors to form a variety of new colors. Little white fuzzies lined their stems instead of thorns. Jimmy spotted what must have been moonflowers, judging by their wedge shapes, with long leaves sprouting little tongues that collected dew.

Beebo held his hands out, gesturing at the surroundings. "Jimmy like?" Jimmy was speechless. He wondered if he'd stepped into one of Oma's books. He stood up and started walking around slowly, to catch every detail.

Long-stemmed plant bulbs funneled bubbles that floated around his head. When they popped, a tiny spray of perfume exploded and quickly dissolved, which created a wonderfully sweet aroma. "Our farm doesn't smell anything like *this*!" said Jimmy.

The tree trunks were covered in wild colors, such as pink and magenta, some with unusual plaid or spotted patterns. Some tree trunks had podlike things growing on them.

They were soft to the touch, and when Jimmy bumped into one, he bounced off as if it was a cushion. The leaves hanging overhead looked as if they'd been painted every color, and some trees had hair instead of leaves. Long strands hung down almost to the ground, and they tickled Jimmy's neck as he passed underneath. Bushes and shrubs competed for attention with foliage in bright, fluorescent pinks and yellows.

Beebo cut some strands from the hair of a tree, bound them around the end of a small stick, dipped it in a coconut shell that contained a red liquid, and handed it to Jimmy. "A paintbrush!" said Jimmy. "You're putting me to work?!"

Beebo shook his head. "Play!" A dozen coconut shells sat on a tree stump, each filled with different colors of paint. Beebo pointed to a nearby pine tree. Then he took another brush and, with a deft series of strokes, splashed blue paint onto the trunk of a hazel tree. He bounced on his tail and hummed a little tune as he slapped the paint around in broad, sweeping strokes. Carelessly dipping the brush from one shell to another, and creating quite a mess on the ground, Beebo made bold swirling lines.

Jimmy watched Beebo briefly, and then, with great hesitation, he lifted the brush to the tree. Very carefully, with slow, timid brush strokes, Jimmy made a stripe, straight up and down. He was quite proud that he kept the line an even thickness, and so he started a second stripe, leaving an equally wide gap in between. With painstaking exactness, Jimmy meticulously copied the first stripe. Then he made another, and another, working his way around the tree.

Beebo studied Jimmy's work. With folded arms, and head slightly tilted, Beebo rubbed two fingers across his lips. "Hmmmm," he muttered, wiping his paint-stained hands on his tummy. He grabbed Jimmy's hand and dragged his brush along the tree, making quick, darting motions. "Make loosy-goosy arms!" he said. "Dancy-fancy, dainty-painty!"

Jimmy tried what Beebo suggested, but his brush strokes were still rigid and mechanical, and he couldn't seem to paint anything but straight lines. Beebo tickled him under his arms. Jimmy giggled and squirmed, and his brush made a squiggly line. "Look what you made me do!" he said, slightly annoyed, and resumed painting straight lines.

Beebo shook his head. "Try paint with wiggly fingers?"

The idea seemed silly to Jimmy, but he carefully dipped the tip of his forefinger in some blue paint and made a narrow, straight line on the tree trunk. Beebo lost his patience then. He grabbed Jimmy's wrists and plunged both the boy's hands entirely in two different paint shells. Then he dragged them all around the tree trunk, making the lines overlap and the colors blend together. "Splashy-dashy, silly-nilly!" he uttered.

"Hey, hey!!" Jimmy protested. "Be careful!! Look at my shirt!" A few spots of red paint had splattered onto Jimmy's shirt. Beebo shook his head, and with a casual flick of his brush, sprayed a dozen paint drops onto Jimmy's shirt, and his pants as well.

"Hey!" Jimmy angrily eyed Beebo.

Beebo mocked Jimmy's attitude, huffing and puffing loudly. Then he sprayed Jimmy from head to toe with paint, then scurried playfully behind a tree. Waddling like a duck, he comically swayed back and forth, with his long tail dragging behind, and Jimmy had to laugh. But he wasn't about to let Beebo get away with that. He dipped his brush

deep into some green paint and splashed Beebo across the tummy. Beebo quickly shot a spray of bright yellow as Jimmy ran for cover. Back and forth it went, quickly developing into an all-out paint war.

Several hours later, Beebo lay in the grass. A long weed hung from his lips, and a coconut paint shell sat on his head like a hat. His entire body was covered with paint of every color imaginable, and so was Jimmy's. He stood nearby, putting the final touches of his masterpiece on the trunk of a weeping willow—a bright green house that leaned crookedly to one side, with loose hanging shutters and a lopsided chimney that spouted pink, square-shaped puffs of smoke. A purple cat peered hungrily at two gigantic orange milk bottles that stood, one on top of the other, on a red doormat, which said in big yellow letters: VELCOME.

"Bravo! Fantastico!" said Beebo, genuinely impressed.

"I can't believe I made that!" Jimmy turned to Beebo and laughed. "You're a mess!"

Beebo chuckled and leaped into the stream with a magnificent splash. In seconds he resurfaced and gestured for Jimmy to join him. Jimmy took off his T-shirt and overalls and made a cannonball jump. He sank to the bottom and opened his eyes. The rocks and plants glittered from the reflecting sunlight. Several fish swam right up to his face, and he smiled at them. The water felt warm, and as Jimmy floated to the surface he noticed the paint dissolving off his skin. He grabbed his clothes and pulled them into the water. The paint dissolved, and Jimmy laid them on the grass to dry.

Beebo floated peacefully on his back. Jimmy climbed onto Beebo's big belly. His skin and clothes were washed clean. As Jimmy admired his painted tree, a thought crossed his mind. "Hey Beebo, what happens when it rains?"

Unconcerned, Beebo shrugged his shoulders and said, "Paint new pictures?"

"That's sad. All that work for nothing," said Jimmy.

"Not for nothing! Paint goes from the tree, but picture stays in your head."

"Oh." Jimmy looked around at all the trees, and the flowers and plants as well, to lock the images in his mind. The setting sun cast a red glow over the scene, which made a magical effect. "This is definitely not like the farm," he mused. Then he jumped up with a jolt. "The farm!" he shouted. "I gotta go!!"

12

Time to Explain

Moments later, Jimmy stood at the back door of his house. "There he is now!" his mother shouted as he entered the house apprehensively.

Mr. Dabble was speaking into the telephone. "Never mind, officer. He just walked in!" Then he hung up.

"Thank goodness!" cried Mrs. Dabble, as she took Jimmy in her arms.

"We've been looking for you all day, son!" said Mr. Dabble with relief in his voice. "Where have you been?"

Jimmy looked at his mother briefly, then his eyes turned

away to the floor. He tried to talk, but no words came from his mouth. "Jimmy?" Mrs. Dabble led him to a chair and sat him down. "We're happy to see you're okay," she said.

"But we must know where you've been," added Mr. Dabble. In a corner of the room Jimmy spotted Oma. She remained perfectly still.

"What is it, Jimmy?" said Mrs. Dabble. Jimmy looked up toward his parents, but he kept his gaze fixed on a crack in the ceiling behind them to avoid making eye contact. He nervously dragged his shoes back and forth across the floor, shrugged his shoulders, and hemmed and hawed. But he couldn't say anything.

"You can tell us, Jimmy," said Mr. Dabble quietly.

"The boy must be hungry," said Oma. "Can he haf something . . ."

"As soon as he tells us where he's been, Ma."

"Uhm," Jimmy mumbled, but that was all he could muster.

"Maybe you need to think about it in your room?" added Mr. Dabble.

Jimmy nodded and ran up the stairs to his room. Happy to avoid his parents, he hopped onto his bed and lay perfectly still, while his heart beat fast. What am I going to do? he wondered. He felt bad for disobeying his parents, and yet he didn't want to tell them about Beebo. The more he thought about it, the more tired he felt.

An hour later Mr. and Mrs. Dabble came up to talk to Jimmy, but he was sound asleep. "We'll talk with him in the morning," said Mr. Dabble, and they went back downstairs. Jimmy snored peacefully. Dreams floated in and out of his head. Vivid colors in wild shapes changed constantly and moved in slow motion. A slight smile crossed Jimmy's face, and for the time being he was safe.

When Mrs. Dabble checked on Jimmy in the morning, he

was still sleeping. She quietly left the room, and a few moments later Jimmy opened his eyes. He was still in that wondrous state, not fully asleep and not quite awake, and he tried in vain to recall his dreams. All he could see were fuzzy details, but it was enough to make him think that up till now his dreams had all been in black-and-white.

He sat up and stared at the picture on the wall of the boy with his arms stretched over his head. He tipped the picture sideways, which made the boy appear to be flying. With a satisfied nod, Jimmy hopped out of bed and bounded down the stairs. His parents and Oma were having breakfast in the kitchen. Jimmy waltzed to his seat and greeted them with a perky, "Happy-dappy morning, everyone! I'm ready for a humdumdinger day!"

The others stared at him with wide eyes. "Hmmmmm!" Jimmy uttered with a great, big smile, "Oatmeal! Yummy-yummy for my tummy!" He filled his bowl, took a quick bite, and declared, "Mmm, mmm! *Deeeeelicious* in a most *tasty* way!"

Mr. and Mrs. Dabble stared at him with dumbfounded expressions, but Jimmy went on undeterred. "Thanky-danky, Mom! Most considerate of you. A good breakfast is *so* important for a productive day!!"

Mr. Dabble put his spoon down and stared openmouthed.

Jimmy gulped his oatmeal, which seemed to energize him, because he was talking faster and louder. "Mending the fence today, right-o, Pop? Need a little handy-dandy help? Together we'll have that ol' fence completo in no time-o!"

Oma watched Jimmy with a grand smile that stretched from ear to ear. But Mr. and Mrs. Dabble were less enthused. "What's gotten into you?" his mother gasped.

"Just happy-dappy to do my chorios!" sang Jimmy, and with his mouth full of oatmeal, he hopped off his chair.

He'd nearly reached the door when his father said, "Just a minute, son."

Jimmy turned and bellowed, "Right-o, Pop!"

"Have a seat, Jimmy," said Mrs. Dabble with a stern face.

Jimmy slowly returned to his chair, sensing that his parents weren't sharing his buoyant mood. Oma wheeled herself away from the table, muttering, "I go to my room. I haf a book on Puerto Rico, I must go and seek . . . o!"

Jimmy and his parents turned toward Oma. "Ha! That rhymes!" she exclaimed before disappearing down the hall.

Jimmy giggled, but then he saw his parents' serious gaze. "Just where were you yesterday?" Mr. Dabble said.

Jimmy looked down at the table, avoiding his parents' eyes. "We looked everywhere for you," said his mother.

"You missed *all* your afternoon chores!" added Mr. Dabble, his voice rising in anger. Jimmy could see it was no use delaying. It was time to face the music.

"I went to the woods and I saw the strangest creature I've ever seen and his name is Beebo and—"

His parents gasped in unison. "You went into the Dark Woods?!"

Mr. Dabble stood up straight, too angry to know what to do. "We should wash your mouth out with soap, young man!" Then he mumbled, "But that's a waste of soap." He looked at Mrs. Dabble.

She looked back, then stated, "We're grounding you, Jimmy."

"To the farm for the rest of the summer!" Mr. Dabble agreed.

"Until school starts," added Mrs. Dabble.

"Mom! The woods are nothing like you think!" pleaded Jimmy. "And I've *got* to see Beebo again!"

"What's Beebo?!" his parents asked.

"Beebo is my friend in the woods."

"No, son. You're grounded," said Mrs. Dabble, sighing heavily.

"That's final!" stated Mr. Dabble flatly.

"And no more talk of Bobee!" added Mrs. Dabble.

"Beebo," Jimmy uttered sadly.

13

Chores, Chores, and More Chores

"Life is not a fairy tale, Jimmy," said Mrs. Dabble that night before bed. "Your pa and I work very hard to make a good life for us, and your runnin' off like that doesn't help us any. Aren't you a little old for make-believe creatures?" Jimmy stared glumly at the patches on his bedspread. His mother sat down beside him on the bed and put her arm around Jimmy's shoulders. "You've got to learn to be responsible, son," she said with a heavy sigh. "We're givin' you extra chores. Bedtime will be eight o'clock sharp, and let's hold off on readin' time with Oma for a spell, until you prove you can handle it, okay?"

Jimmy slowly nodded his head.

The next morning, Mrs. Dabble gave Jimmy a math book she'd gotten from his teacher and taped a schedule of daily assignments on the refrigerator. "This'll keep you occupied. If you complete five pages every day, you'll finish the book by summer's end." She stuck a pencil in Jimmy's hand and said, "Hop to it."

Jimmy plopped down at the kitchen table and stared at the book. Math was his worst subject at school. What a bum deal! he thought. His whole summer was ruined. Worst of all, he couldn't see Beebo again. He angrily tapped his pencil on the tabletop.

"Get going, Jimmy," prodded his mother from the hallway. "Time's a wastin'!"

Pouting, Jimmy opened the math book. Thirty tedious minutes later, he finished the first assignment. Mrs. Dabble put a check mark on the schedule and sent Jimmy to the chicken coop. The animals sensed his bad mood and left him alone. With his head hung low, he collected the eggs.

As Jimmy raked the straw in straight, even strokes, he remembered Beebo's painting lesson. His heart sank. He changed his pattern, raking in circular motions, until he'd formed a big round pile. And then he got an idea. He ran into the barn and returned with a shovel and started digging.

An hour later, Jimmy's parents checked on his progress. They peered inside the chicken coop and found the straw stacked into the shape of a castle. A drawbridge crossed the moat that surrounded the castle. The chickens marched back and forth by the entrance like soldiers, wearing bottle caps for helmets. Mr. Dabble took the pipe from his mouth and gave a deep sigh. Mrs. Dabble frowned. Suddenly a

loud commotion startled them. They rushed to the front yard, where a dozen sheep were frolicking on their backs in the grass. Jimmy sat on the little gate, cheering them on.

"I told you to rake the leaves, Jimmy," Mrs. Dabble gasped. "Now get to work!"

"But look, Mom," replied Jimmy. But his parents walked away without seeing that the leaves were sticking to the sheep's wool. Within minutes the yard was clear. Jimmy simply raked the leaves from the sheep's backs into the trash can.

After lunch Mr. Dabble was patching a tractor tire when a sheep missing half its wool ran by. "What in tarnation?" He rushed after her, and with the sheep in his arms, Mr. Dabble marched toward the barn. There was Jimmy, standing beside the cow. "Did you shear this sheep, Jimmy?" he demanded.

"Yes, Pa," replied Jimmy. "That's Sharon. She was really insecure because she looked just like all the other sheep. So I cut a flower design in her wool."

Mr. Dabble put Sharon down and studied her. Her wool *was* in the shape of a tulip. "And see what I did with the wool?!" Jimmy proudly pointed to Suzy, who was sporting a large woolen glove over her udder. "That way her milk will keep warm," Jimmy explained.

Dumbfounded, Mr. Dabble set the sheep down. "Don't cut any more wool," he said as he walked away. "And finish your chores!"

Jimmy fed Al and swept the driveway, and then he snuck into Oma's room to tell her about his invention for Suzy's udder. "That's usink your thinkink cap!" she squealed. "The Barber of Seville" blared from the radio, and Oma explained the music to Jimmy. Together they sang along. Oma was horribly out of key, but it gave Jimmy a terrific idea.

An hour later Mrs. Dabble stepped outside to ring the dinner bell. "Where is that music coming from?" she asked herself. She followed the sound to the chicken coop, where a transistor radio was blasting Vivaldi's "Four Seasons." "Don't waste batteries on chickens, Jimmy!"

"But Janet needs to lay more eggs, Ma. I heard you say so yourself! The music will help Janet relax, I'm sure of it!"

"Really, Jimmy," Mrs. Dabble grumbled as she shut off the radio. "If God wanted chickens to appreciate music, he would've given them ears!" And she walked away without even noticing that the power of suggestion had indeed caused Janet to lay several eggs.

Suzy's milk production doubled that afternoon. Jimmy brought two full milk buckets into the kitchen, but his parents were busy talking and didn't see it. "Why can't you do things the normal way?" Mrs. Dabble asked Jimmy during supper.

"Like you *used* to do!" added Mr. Dabble.

"I don't understand what's come over you, Jimmy," said his mother. Jimmy shrugged, then launched into a tale about Al the pig's weight problem. Oma smiled without saying a word.

The next morning Jimmy finished his math assignment in precisely twenty minutes. After feeding the chickens, he planted flowers around their coop. Then he fed Al and poured soap into his mud so he could take a bubble bath. Jimmy led the animals in a walk around the farm and—despite protests from the chickens—started them doing daily calisthenics. Jimmy's parents looked on from the cornfield, shaking their heads. "I've got to find out what's wrong with that boy," said Mr. Dabble.

The next day Jimmy's mother took him to the family doctor, but he couldn't find anything wrong with Jimmy. "I don't understand him anymore, Doctor," said Mrs. Dabble wearily. "Yesterday I found him sitting on the cow's back, playing checkers with a chicken! He painted a checkerboard over her spots!" She gave a heavy sigh. "Tomorrow is his birthday. Is this any way for a nine-year-old to act?"

"He might be going through a stage right now, Maggie," said Dr. Ballgladder, rubbing his bushy mustache. "Why don't you ease up on him a bit? Let him enjoy his birthday."

14

Jimmy's Birthday

The following morning, Mrs. Dabble made flapjacks for breakfast. Beside Jimmy's plate lay a present, wrapped in newspaper, with a red bow on top. Jimmy carefully removed the bow and handed it to his mother. Then he tore away the newspaper to find a brand-new cowboy hat, a sheriff's star, and a water pistol. "Thanks, Ma and Pa!" exclaimed Jimmy excitedly. Mr. and Mrs. Dabble nodded happily, even though they couldn't really spare the money. The hat was too big for Jimmy's head, but it had been on sale. And the pistol was actually a space gun, which didn't fit the cowboy theme, but Jimmy didn't care. Oma gave him her copy of *Wagons Ho—The Westward Trail* and a chocolate bar, and they all sang happy birthday to Jimmy.

Jimmy hungrily gulped down his pancakes when there came a knock at the door. "That'll be Fred," said Mr. Dabble, wiping syrup from his mouth. "Happy birthday, Jimmy. Me and Mr. Daly are gonna fix the barn loft."

Mr. Daly, a kindly, heavyset man, owned a large farm up the road. Jimmy's father left the house and went into the barn with Mr. Daly. "Finish your breakfast, Sheriff Jimmy," said Mrs. Dabble as she cleared the table. "I reckon there are bandits out there that need roundin' up!"

"Yes, ma'am," replied Jimmy in a slow drawl. "I'll protect you womenfolk! Don't you worry none!" He tied a napkin around his neck and shoved a final forkful of pancake into his mouth.

"Hurry, sheriff!" Oma said. "Those bandits haf robbed the bank, and they are gettink avay!"

"It's my sworn duty to uphold the law!" proclaimed Jimmy bravely. He took a bite of his chocolate bar and carefully rewrapped it and tucked it in his pocket. Then he grabbed his fully loaded, dripping gun, pulled his hat down low over his forehead, and stepped outside in a tough-guy swagger.

"You get those bad guys and clean the town up vit them, sheriff!" Oma shouted after him.

Jimmy headed toward the chicken coop and circled around back. Janet, Joy, and Bridget were chatting up a storm. Jimmy snuck up from behind and surprised them. "Well, well, well, well," he said, casually leaning against the side of the coop. "If it ain't the notorious redhead gang!"

The chickens stopped talking instantly and stared at Jimmy. "The game's up, folks!" Jimmy bellowed. "Hand over them eggs, and no funny business!"

Janet squawked, and Jimmy pointed his squirt gun at her. "Reach for the sky!" he demanded, "and make it snappy, sister!"

The chickens gasped. Just then Al came by. Jimmy jumped sideways. "Aha, thought you could get the jump on me, did ya?!" he shouted and squirt the poor pig smack on the snout. Al was momentarily caught offguard, but then he dropped back and beautifully faked a melodramatic death. Jimmy turned to the coop, and fired away at the hapless chickens, who ran in circles squawking at the top of their lungs.

Jimmy fell to the ground laughing. Al laughed so hard, he started coughing. "You should be ashamed of yourself, young man!" squawked Bridget.

"Scaring ladies of advanced age!" mumbled Joy.

"Speak for yourself, deary," clucked Bridget angrily, shaking the water from her back end. "Just look at me! I'm a mess! I try to keep up appearances!"

"Oh stop your yammering, Bridget!" Janet couldn't suppress a laugh, even though she was soaked herself. "Hey, I'm back on track laying eggs, Jimmy!"

"Yes! We've got that song from the radio memorized," said Joy. "C'mon, girls, let's sing a round for Jimmy!" Suzy joined the troop, and with Janet and Joy they began humming the melody from *Rigoletto*. Bridget continued to complain until Janet nudged her, and she grudgingly joined in.

Suddenly Joy laid an egg. "See? It's affecting us *all*!" she clucked happily. Then Al tried to hum along, but his voice croaked horribly, which brought the singing to an abrupt end.

Half an hour later Mrs. Dabble found Jimmy in the pantry, nursing his pig with a bottle of milk. "Jimmy!" she said sternly. "Need I remind you that milk is precious? We can't waste it on a pig! I know it's your birthday and all, but we *do* have rules."

"But it's *absolutely* necessary," Jimmy assured her. "Al is sick!"

"What's the matter with him?" asked his mother apprehensively.

"He has a sore throat," replied Jimmy.

"How do you know?" she asked incredulously.

"He can't hit a G-sharp!" Jimmy prompted Al, who made several gravelly oinks. Jimmy sadly turned to his mother. "See?"

Mrs. Dabble managed a smile, but she took the bottle away nevertheless, and sent Al outside. But the pig felt better already, and that afternoon Jimmy sat on Al's back, bouncing in a makeshift saddle he rigged onto the pig's back. Twirling a lasso over his head, Jimmy shouted, "Get along, li'l Suzy!" as Al chased the old cow around the front yard. The chickens ran along beside them, squawking with excitement.

Suzy darted into the barn, with Al in hot pursuit, and they nearly collided with Jimmy's father, who was handling a big electric saw. Mr. Dabble was quite upset. "Keep that hog away, Jimmy!" he shouted.

"Sorry, Pa," replied Jimmy, and he quickly led the animals outside. Then he peered into the barn. Mr. Daly was holding a large sheet of plywood which Mr. Dabble struggled to cut. The electric saw stalled, started up again, and then stopped. Jimmy could see the frustration on his father's face.

"What's with this blasted thing?!" snapped Mr. Dabble.

After several more power surges, Mr. Daly said, "It ain't the saw, Hank. You got electrical problems! This ol' barn needs rewiring."

"That'll cost an arm and a leg!" replied Mr. Dabble, wiping the sweat from his forehead. "I'll fix it myself."

Jimmy quietly tiptoed away and made sure Al kept out of his father's sight for the rest of the day. By supper time Mr. Dabble's mood had improved. To wrap up Jimmy's birthday, Mrs. Dabble made corn dogs with French fries, and Oma told some funny stories. Jimmy went to bed with a smile on his face. But he had no idea of the shock that awaited him.

15

Hard Times

That night, as he lay in bed, Jimmy overheard his parents arguing. He quietly crawled to the edge of the banister at the top of the stairs, keeping himself out of sight. Below him sat his mother, knitting socks by a dim light, while Mr. Dabble stood by the fireplace. "The tractor needs a new fuel pump, chicken wire in the coop needs replacing . . ."

"We can tighten our belts a bit more," said Mrs. Dabble.

"Last month's bank payment was late, and there's barely enough for this month's, Mag."

"We could sell the figurine collection. That should fetch a—"

"Absolutely not!" Mr. Dabble cut in. "That's *yours* and always will be!"

There was a long silence, and then Mrs. Dabble said, "Market day isn't far off. We've got to sell the wool early this year, and get top price . . ."

"I say the pig goes to the butcher!" said Mr. Dabble.

Jimmy gasped in shock. "Jimmy will be heartbroken, Hank. It's his pig."

"Listen, Maggie, that pig is eating us out of house and home!"

"Do you remember when Jimmy was six? He was *begging* us for a puppy, and you told him he didn't need one because that pig followed him around everywhere like a dog."

Mr. Dabble sighed. "The farm is more important than the pig," he said, strumming his fingers on the mantel out of agitation. "I'll take the pig early tomorrow morning, before Jimmy wakes up." Mrs. Dabble remained silent, and Mr. Dabble added, "I'll talk to him when I get back."

Jimmy was horrified. The thought of Al going to the butcher was too dreadful for words. He lay awake all night scheming ways to save his pig. By dawn he'd dreamt up a plan, and got out his brushes and some red paint.

Jimmy was sleeping soundly by the time Mr. Dabble left the house to fetch Al. But his plans were dashed when he found the pig flat on his back, legs in the air, with his belly completely covered in red dots. Al let out a low, painful groan. "Shoot!" said Mr. Dabble, scratching his head with his pipe. "You won't fetch much lookin' like that!"

Back in the house he said to Mrs. Dabble, "Guess I won't be going to the butcher today."

"Good heavens, why not?"

"That darn thing's gone and come down with the measles!"

Jimmy knew his plan was only a temporary solution, so he put Al on a fitness program. Under Jimmy's strict supervision, Al did deep knee bends, sit-ups, and jumping jacks three times a day, and he trimmed down nicely. Mr. Dabble made several other attempts to take him to the butcher, but Jimmy sabotaged his plans each time.

To save money the Dabbles ate half rations for supper. Lights were rarely on, everyone bathed once less per week, and Oma played her radio only every other day. Jimmy tried to do his part, too. He was milking Suzy when his father stopped by. "Dang blast it! Now we gotta call in the vet. Just look at that brown milk comin' out of that old cow!"

"No, Pa!" exclaimed Jimmy, "I've found a way to make some extra money! Natural chocolate milk, straight from the udder!"

"Chocolate milk?" replied his father, slightly baffled.

"I fed Suzy the rest of my chocolate bar this morning!" Jimmy said excitedly, quite proud of his accomplishment.

"What do you think you're doin' ruining perfectly good milk? Will you just stop tryin' to help, Jimmy?!"

Tears welled in Jimmy's eyes, and he ran off to the chicken coop. Janet, Joy, and Bridget were there. "Nothing I do is right!" Jimmy lamented, and he explained what had happened with Suzy's milk.

"That's too bad, Jimmy," said Janet. "They just don't understand."

"I'm sorry, Jimmy. My parents didn't always understand me either," said Bridget.

"And with good reason," cackled Joy.

"Just what's that supposed to mean?!" countered Bridget.

Janet stepped between the arguing hens. "Now now, girls, we're trying to help Jimmy, remember?" She turned to Jimmy and said, "I'll bet you'd like to go visit Beebo right now."

Jimmy nodded. "I was free to do whatever I wanted with Beebo in the woods."

Suzy joined the group, with Al on her heels and several sheep behind him. "I don't understand your parents, Jimmy," said Suzy. "They complain about wasting, and then they throw away perfectly good milk! As if I can produce it by the hour!"

"It makes no sense," agreed Jimmy.

Mr. Dabble walked by with the washed milk bucket in his hand. Still upset about the chocolate milk, he bent down and leaned into the coop. "They can't understand you, son," he said. "Animals are dumb."

"They are *not*!" Jimmy replied defensively.

But Mr. Dabble shook his head as he walked away, saying, "The broom closet needs sweeping."

Oma appeared from behind a tree and approached

Jimmy with a sympathetic smile. She had watched the whole scene. "Your folks are havink a hard time right now, Jimmy," she said while rolling her chair between two sheep. "Sometimes people haf to vork things out for themselves. Just keep doink your best at vat you do."

"Thank you, Oma," said Jimmy quietly, and the animals nodded in agreement.

"Say, vhy don't you and the animals put on a show!" Oma smiled brightly at her own suggestion. "That should cheer your folks up a bit!"

"That's a great idea!" said Jimmy.

16

A Big Show

Several days went by without incident. The mood around the Dabble farm had become quite dreary. But Jimmy kept himself busy. Inspired by Oma's suggestion, he'd begun writing an opera about the perils of a young chicken named Prima Rivera, who fought off the advances of a nasty old rooster named Raviolo. The rooster's evil intent was to steal Prima Rivera's father's fortune. Oma gave Jimmy a harmonica, which helped him to create some lovely melodies.

One morning Jimmy gathered the animals in the barn to rehearse Act One. He sat on the old tractor and announced in a proper British accent he'd heard on the radio, "Ladies and gentlemen, we have a great show in store for you today! A concerto from the world-famous Dabble Farm Symphony Orchestra! Please save your applause until the end of the show! Lovely!!"

Suzy, playing the role of a gypsy, did a belly dance, keeping a rhythm with the bell that hung around her neck. From the rafters, Joy and Bridget joined in, yodeling a beautiful two-part soprano. A sympathetic sheriff, played by Al, sprang onto a bale of hay, crooning his golden tenor voice. While maintaining her four-legged swivel and humming the soprano part, Suzy stepped up and balanced on Al's back. Al grimaced but held firm.

Then Janet took center stage, juggling three eggs. Playing the part of Prima Rivera, a carefree chicken whom all the roosters had eyes for, she sang about finding true love. Janet worked her way from Al's rump onto Suzy's back, where the light from a window threw a spotlight on her. Bridget and Joy leapt onto Suzy's horns, bowing to Janet in melodramatic fashion.

"Magnificent!" shouted Jimmy.

At that very moment, Mrs. Dabble happened by. She was carrying a large basket of laundry. The eggs, the chickens, the cow, and the pig . . . it was too much for her. She

116

stormed into the barn, shouting, *"What's going on here?!"*

Startled, Suzy reared up, sending the chickens tumbling from her back, and from there it all went terribly wrong. Janet somehow managed to catch an egg on her way down, but the other eggs sailed past her, breaking one after the other on Mrs. Dabble's head. Janet landed on Al, and dug her claws deep into the poor pig's back, giving him such a severe jolt, that he flung himself against the wall, crashing into the garden tools and sending them flying through the barn. While her feet scrambled back and forth on the slippery yolk-covered floor, Mrs. Dabble caught a rake square on the chin, and fell. Suzy landed with a *thud* on Mrs. Dabble's leg, which effectively brought the rehearsal to an end.

Dr. Ballgladder put Mrs. Dabble's leg in a cast and ordered her to stay off it for a month. "I'll send you the bill next week," he said as he made his way out. Jimmy and his father stood around the bed, glumly staring at Mrs. Dabble's leg, which hung suspended by a rope from the ceiling lamp. Mr. Dabble kept his head in his hands.

"I was only trying to make you and Mom happy," Jimmy stammered.

Before anyone could respond, a voice came from the front door. "Mail!"

Mr. Dabble left the room without saying a word while

Jimmy stared sadly at the quilt on his mother's bed. Mr. Dabble returned with a letter in his hand. "It's the bank," he said with little emotion. "If we miss our next payment, they're taking the farm."

Jimmy gasped and ran up to his room.

17

Shearing the Sheep

Jimmy went to bed without supper that night. Wracked with guilt, he couldn't show his face at the table. He slept fitfully through the night, and was still sleeping when the early morning sun came streaming through the window. A squeak from the bedroom door jolted him awake. His father stepped into the room and set a half-filled glass of milk and a sandwich on the nightstand. "Thought you'd be hungry," he said as he sat down on the bed.

Jimmy looked up. "How's Mom?"

"She'll be okay."

Jimmy took a bite of the sandwich. "I was angry at you last night, Jimmy," said Mr. Dabble, "but I know that accidents happen. You meant no harm to your ma." He stared out the window and continued, "It's just that, we're going through some tough times right now, son."

For a moment he was quiet, and Jimmy kept his eyes down. "Big day ahead," said his father. "I could use some help shearin' those sheep."

Jimmy looked up at his dad and said, "I'll be ready in five minutes, Pa!" and he took a big bite from the sandwich.

Market Day—a three-day annual event—was not far off. People came from miles around to buy and sell goods. This was Jimmy's parents' only hope to recoup some of their losses. Although market day was small potatoes for the large farms in the area, this was a big payday for Mr. and Mrs. Dabble.

Jimmy collected the sheep and lined them up single file. To keep them in line he entertained them with a story about a boy's visit to the barbershop. This put the sheep in a good mood, and they cooperated well. By early afternoon nearly half the sheep were shorn. They took a break so Mr. Dabble could go into town to get medicine for his wife. As Jimmy watched his father's truck putter down the hill, he noticed Janet swinging peacefully in a tire that hung from a tree branch. Instantly an idea popped into his head, and he exclaimed, "I'll finish the job for my dad!"

He climbed up the tree and untied the rope from the branch. "Time to get busy, Janet!" he shouted. With a squawk of protest, Janet jumped aside as the tire dropped to the ground. Jimmy dragged the tire into the barn and gathered all the animals around him.

A short while later, the tire hung suspended by two ropes from a ceiling beam in the barn. The ropes were tied to Suzy's horns. Suzy stood in a corner of the barn. Jimmy hopped inside the tire, with shears in hand.

Next to Jimmy was a makeshift platform made with bundles of hay. One sheep after the other leaped up onto the platform, and Jimmy cut its wool with amazing accuracy. The system he had devised allowed Jimmy to change positions with a short command to Suzy. By simply tilting her head, or turning left or right, Suzy pulled the ropes which moved the tire to any position Jimmy desired.

In this manner, Jimmy was able to work very quickly. The sheep stood in a line that reached past the front door of the house, and every minute another one happily strolled out of the barn, sporting a perfect buzz cut. The chickens helped, too. They laid out the wool in a corner of the barn, and Al rolled over it to flatten it out. Then they piled the wool in orderly stacks, so everything was neat and tidy.

As he worked, Jimmy made up a little song, and all the animals hummed along with the melody. The place sounded like a choir of monks doing a turn on Mother Goose.

This little sheep went to market.
This little sheep stayed home.
This little sheep sold all her wool,
But this little sheep had none.
And this little sheep went to the bank,
And saved her little home.

Oma took a break from taking care of Mrs. Dabble. She rolled her wheelchair into the barn and was amazed by what she saw. "Vat a clever idea, Pollyvog!"

"Thanks, Oma!" Jimmy shouted back. "Won't Dad be surprised?"

"Vat?" shouted Oma, who was surrounded by sheep humming Jimmy's nursery rhyme.

"I said, won't Dad be surprised?"

"You bet!" replied Oma, adding, "Sure is dark in there!" She flicked the light switch on and off several times.

"No, Oma!" shouted Jimmy. "Don't touch that switch! The lamp's bro—"

But Oma didn't hear him. Sparks blew from the lamp. One of them landed underneath the tractor, where a puddle of oil had formed, which instantly caught on fire. The flames quickly spread to the stacks of wool and hay nearby.

"*Watch out, Oma!!*" Jimmy screamed. The animals panicked, pushing and shoving their way out of the barn. Oma's wheelchair was knocked on its side, with Oma trapped underneath. Jimmy jumped to the ground among the frightened sheep and struggled to straighten the wheelchair, but it was too heavy. Oma gasped for air. Jimmy pulled her from the chair and dragged her out of the barn to a clear place.

He watched helplessly as the fire spread, when cries came from inside the barn. "Suzy!" shouted Jimmy.

He darted back into the smoky furnace and found the panic-stricken cow entangled in the ropes. Jimmy climbed onto her back and frantically struggled for several anxious moments. At last the ropes loosened from Suzy's horns, and they scrambled out of the barn. Suzy bolted after the other animals, and Jimmy dropped to the ground, sucking in air. Nearby was his grandmother, lying on her side. As the barn was consumed by fire, Jimmy shook Oma gently, but she didn't move at all.

"Wake up, Oma!" Jimmy desperately shook her, but there was no response. Then the tractor gas tank blew, sending boards and debris flying. A fireball shot up in the sky, and Jimmy threw himself across Oma.

18

Leaving Home

Oma lay on the bed beside Mrs. Dabble, who leaned forward as far as her suspended leg would allow, looking on with teary eyes. Mr. Dabble stood next to Oma, holding her hand. A mask covered Oma's face. A tube connected the mask to a respirator machine, which helped her breathe. Doctor Ballgladder stood nearby, carefully observing the gauges on the machine. All was quiet except for the rhythmic sucking and puffing sounds made by the respirator. Jimmy sat on the floor in the corner, looking on.

"Will she make it, doctor?" asked Mrs. Dabble softly.

"She's inhaled a lot of smoke, Maggie," replied Doctor Ballgladder. He gave Mr. Dabble instructions in caring for Oma, and packed up his things. Mr. Dabble walked him out to the gate. The sun was setting, and dark clouds were creeping into view. Jimmy looked out the window. Firemen had left the ground a wet, muddy mess. The animals were huddled together in a sorry state near the scorched remains of Oma's wheelchair. His dad stood amid the ruins of his barn, staring at the smoldering pile of metal that was his

tractor. He picked a blackened shred of wool off the fender, kicked a burnt bucket, and went back inside.

Jimmy cringed as his father stood in the doorway. "You!" he commanded. "Come here!"

Mrs. Dabble motioned for her husband to keep calm. Jimmy stepped past his father into the hallway. Mr. Dabble nearly shook with anger, and his gaze scared Jimmy. "Upstairs!!" he seethed. "I want you out of my sight!"

Sobbing, Jimmy scrambled to his bedroom and dropped down on his bed. He lay there as his father's bitter words drifted up through the open window. Trying to control his tears, Jimmy leaned close to the window and listened. "We're ruined!" Mr. Dabble growled. "My tractor, the wool's destroyed! The doctor bills alone will bankrupt us!!"

"Are we such failures as parents, Harry?" asked Mrs. Dabble.

"We weren't strict enough with him."

Jimmy stared at the ceiling as he listened. A numbness knotted in his gut. He quietly got up and broke open his piggy bank and placed the contents next to his pillow. It added up to four dollars and thirteen cents, which he'd saved from an allowance Oma had given him. He wrote a note for his parents that said:

Dear Mom and Dad,

I'm sorry for all the problems I've caused you. I'm a bad son, and I won't trouble you anymore.

Good-bye, Jimmy

Jimmy left the note on his pillow beside the money and filled a knapsack with some books, his squirt gun, and a flashlight. Then he put on a sturdy jacket and, using his bedsheets as a rope, climbed out the window. As he snuck past the remains of the barn, Jimmy took a final look at the house, then turned and ran into the darkness.

19

Beebo

Jimmy ran through the woods, screaming Beebo's name. He stumbled through the foliage until his legs felt as though they would give out, when Beebo appeared. Jimmy burst into tears and told Beebo what had happened. Beebo put his arms around Jimmy and sat down on the ground. "I've ruined everything, Beebo! I'm no good. I want to stay here with you."

For a while Beebo was quiet. Then he looked off, and said, "Why do the chickens lay many flibbers?" His voice was calm and quiet, and very different from before.

Jimmy watched Beebo, surprised by the change in his voice, but he didn't answer. "How much framooo does the cow make?" Beebo continued. "Are not the sheep helpful to Jimmy's mom and dad? Those things are because of Jimmy. Jimmy made his Oma happy and helped his mom and dad in many ways. They do not know it yet."

Jimmy looked away and sighed. Beebo put a finger to Jimmy's chin and turned his head back. He gazed deep into Jimmy's eyes and said, "Jimmy is running from his problems."

"You think I should go back?"

Beebo nodded.

"I can't!" cried Jimmy.

"Yes, you can. Beebo go with Jimmy."

"You will?"

Beebo smiled. "But first eat." He gathered some plants and fruit and started eating. Jimmy watched him without touching the food. "Jimmy need strength for what's to come!"

"What's to come, then?"

Beebo didn't reply. He set some yellow beans in Jimmy's lap and nudged his hand. Jimmy sighed and picked up the beans and put one in his mouth.

Later that night, two silhouettes zoomed up the hill toward the Dabble farm. Beebo set Jimmy down by the gate and gazed at the remains of the barn. The house was dark and quiet. Even the animals were asleep. Beebo told Jimmy quietly to call them, and a few minutes later they were all gathered together, staring wide-eyed at Beebo. "Jimmy told us all about you," said Bridget, slightly blushing.

"Sorry we couldn't meet under better circumstances," said Janet sadly.

"It's a shame what's happened here," added Suzy.

"Beebo has a plan," whispered Jimmy, "and we need all of your help."

The animals perked up, eager to do their part. Beebo stepped into the middle and began assigning tasks. With plenty of light from the moon, they quietly set to work. Suzy pulled lumber with ropes tied to her horns, Al held beams in place and carried wood on his back, and the chickens brought nails to Jimmy, as well as helping with the measuring. The sheep stood on top of one another to guide beams into place. Jimmy hammered and sawed, and Beebo was everywhere, barking orders and making things happen with incredible speed.

Just before dawn there stood a nearly completed barn in the same spot the old one was. Suzy and the sheep painted its sides in a freestyle manner in bright green, while the chickens colored the roof in orange and vermilion. Above the doors, in bold yellow letters, was the word VELCOME. The first rays of sunlight touched the barn, making a dazzling sight. Jimmy was straddled on the roof, attaching the weather vane, the only piece that survived the fire unscathed. Beebo sat down beside him. "I can't believe we've done this, Beebo," gushed Jimmy. "You're incredible!"

"You have many talents, Jimmy Dabble," replied Beebo. "You must learn to use them."

"I'm trying. Hey, can you hand me some nails?"

"No, Beebo must go." Jimmy turned to Beebo, who continued. "Jimmy is ready."

"I guess we're nearly done, all right."

"Beebo must leave now."

"Okay. Thanks for your help, Beebo." Jimmy wiped his forehead and continued hammering. "I'll visit you soon."

"No. Jimmy must stay with family. Jimmy doesn't need Beebo anymore." Confused, Jimmy watched Beebo, when the sound of a door slamming startled him. He turned to look at the house. Behind him Beebo said quietly, "Goodbye, Jimmy Dabble."

20

Starting Over

The front door opened, and Mr. Dabble rushed outside with a worried face. Jimmy's note was in his hand. Jimmy turned back to Beebo, but he was already gone. Mr. Dabble ran to his truck. From behind he heard, "Hey, Pa, what do you think?"

Mr. Dabble looked around, spotted the barn, and stumbled back. "Up here, Dad!" Jimmy waved.

Mr. Dabble just stood and stared, unable to find the words to speak. Jimmy climbed down from the barn and joined his father. "You like it, Dad?"

"How did you . . . what did you . . . I don't understand," Mr. Dabble mumbled.

Jimmy shrugged humbly. "The animals were a big help."

As if in a daze, Mr. Dabble approached the barn. He tapped the sides, shook some beams, and swung the doors a few times. It was sturdy and well put together. "Jimmy, I . . ." He still couldn't find the words. At last he handed Jimmy the note and, rubbing his hair, said, "I'm glad you're back, son."

Then they headed into the house. Together they made breakfast, without a word spoken between them. When Mrs. Dabble woke up, Jimmy brought her some food. Oma lay still beside her. The respirator machine puffed noisily nearby. As Mr. Dabble entered the room, Mrs. Dabble said, "What's wrong, Hank? You're white as a sheet!"

Mr. Dabble slowly walked to the window and parted the curtains, revealing the brightly colored barn. It had started raining, and a glorious rainbow made the barn glow with life. "Good heavens!" said Mrs. Dabble. "When did—"

"I don't know, Maggie," said Mr. Dabble. "I have no idea."

Mrs. Dabble turned to Jimmy. "What's going on, Jimmy?"

Just then Oma coughed, and her body jerked a few times. Mr. Dabble rushed to her side and removed the breathing tube from her mouth. "Mother! Are you all right?!"

Oma coughed again, and Mr. Dabble helped her sit up. She looked around and bellowed, "Vat are you all starink at me for?"

"Thank goodness you're okay!" said Mrs. Dabble, wiping a tear from her eye. Jimmy rushed over and gave Oma a hug, and Mr. Dabble kissed her on the forehead. The respirator machine was still huffing and puffing, and as Mr. Dabble shut it off, he reminded Oma of the barn fire.

Before Oma could speak, Jimmy quickly said, "It's all my fault, Oma."

Oma coughed a bit and held Jimmy tightly. "You do not need to cover for me, Pollyvog. Don't be cross vit him, Henry. It vas not his fault."

"Of course it was his fault, Mother!" grunted Mr. Dabble.

"No, Henry, you are vrong!" pleaded Oma. "It vas my fault! *I* turned the light switch on!" Occasionally pausing for breath, Oma described how sparks from the light started the fire.

Mr. Dabble's face turned red. "The wiring—never fixed it," he uttered.

Oma went on. "Jimmy tried to varn me, but I did not hear him. It's my fault!" she wept. "I'm very sorry, Henry."

"No, Mother, it's my fault!! I should've spent the money

to . . ." Mr. Dabble took Jimmy in his arms. "I'm sorry, son. All those terrible things I said."

"It doesn't matter, Dad," said Jimmy. "We've got a new barn!" He pointed out the window, so Oma could see his handiwork.

"It's great work, Jimmy, but it doesn't change a thing," said Mr. Dabble, while Oma stared speechlessly at the barn. "We're still broke, and the bank is still going to take the farm!" Still clutching Jimmy, he plopped down on the bed beside his wife. After a long silence, Mr. Dabble said, "We should be glad we're all healthy. We can rent an apartment in town." Controlling his emotions, he added, "I'll find work somewhere."

Jimmy could feel the tension in his father's arms. Mrs. Dabble began to sob, and even Oma had to wipe a few tears. Mr. Dabble got up and left the room. Jimmy watched the two women weep. Then he hopped off the bed, dashed out of the house, and with a determined heart, ran down the hill, disregarding the rain that came gushing down.

He raced into the woods shouting Beebo's name, but there was no sign of him. Jimmy ran on. "Beebo, I need you!" He ran until he found the stream, but it looked different from before. Gone were the colorful flowers and plants, and the strange fruit. It all looked quite ordinary.

137

He barely recognized the waterfall. And the paintings on
the trees had all disappeared. "Beebo!!" shouted Jimmy. He
walked around the area, looking under bushes and plants.
"Beebo, where are you?!"

For a moment Jimmy stood still. Suddenly he understood
Beebo's good-bye earlier that morning. A gush of wind
kicked up, and leaves blew by his face, but he didn't notice.
A long time passed in a matter of moments. Then Jimmy
wiped a tear from his cheek and turned back home.

As he walked up the hill, Jimmy fought the urge to cry.
"It's up to me now," he told himself. And as he thought
about how much he'd miss Beebo, an idea came to him,
and he raced the rest of the way home.

21

A Poultry Love Story

While Oma cared for Mrs. Dabble, and Mr. Dabble dealt with the bank, Jimmy worked on his idea. He prepared the animals, decorated the barn, and drew up posters that he hung all over town and around the valley, announcing:

THE DABBLE FARM PRESENTS

Prima Rivera,
a Little Poultry Love Story

starring
The Dabble Farm Players

A local television station took an interest and aired Jimmy rehearsing the animals, which gave him lots of publicity. From her bed Mrs. Dabble worked the phone, calling all the neighbors, and Oma sewed costumes. Even Mr. Dabble helped out. He built a small stage and a set of bleachers, which Jimmy and Oma decorated with brightly colored streamers.

The big day arrived, and the turnout was phenomenal. People from all over the valley and beyond came to see what all the excitement was about. There was standing room only, and extra tickets were made and quickly sold. Mrs. Dabble had the best seat in the house, front and center, with her leg balanced on a crate. Mr. Dabble sat beside her, with Oma next to him.

The animals performed flawlessly. They mooed and squawked and oinked and baaed. The audience stomped their feet and clapped their hands with the music. They loved the animals. Janet in particular put such emotion into her role of Prima Rivera, the passionate, lovelorn chicken, that the audience was nearly moved to tears. Al wooed the crowd with his soulful tenor voice, and Suzy's dancing entertained everyone. The sheep were bashful and remained in the background. Joy and Bridget, on the other hand, stole the spotlight with their duets as the arguing sisters.

When the show ended, Jimmy received a standing ovation. He had all the animals take bows. His parents were overjoyed, if not a bit dazed by the whole affair. Oma gave Jimmy a hearty hug. "Congrats, Jimmy!" she bellowed. "They loved it!!"

Two journalists interviewed Jimmy, and he credited each and every one of the animals and made sure their names were spelled correctly. Jimmy explained that the event was a fund-raiser. "The bank is going to take our farm from us if we don't make our next payment." The newsmen asked Jimmy lots of questions about the bank and the farm, and he was candid with his answers, which they eagerly jotted down.

Jimmy's picture was in the local paper the next day, and he became the talk of the town. Donations and well wishes came from all over from people who were sympathetic to the Dabble farm cause. By the end of the week, there was enough money to pay the bank. Mr. and Mrs. Dabble had to rub their eyes to believe the amount people gave. Too proud to accept charity, they sent them all some cheese or vegetables.

Wary of bad publicity, the bank had a dramatic change of attitude. They sent a group of men in dark suits to the farm for meetings with Mr. and Mrs. Dabble. Jimmy's parents

were ecstatic about the result. Their monthly payments were cut in half, and the late payments were forgiven.

Stacks of daily mail continued to pour in, which kept Mr. and Mrs. Dabble up into the late hours. That left Jimmy free to run the farm. Under his guidance, Suzy produced far more milk than she ever had. Jimmy fed her butter, which yielded rich buttermilk. And he created a whole line of flavored buttermilks—licorice buttermilk, cotton candy buttermilk, and even a nonfat asparagus buttermilk, which was his least favorite, but a big hit with the city folks. Opera music accompanied Janet, Joy, and Bridget in the chicken coop, and they began laying colored eggs like clockwork. Jimmy taught them to paint lovely designs on them.

The sheep knitted beautiful sweaters from their wool, which Jimmy credited to Oma. Jimmy couldn't shear them fast enough before the new wool appeared, each time in a different color! He even experimented with feeding the sheep a variety of flowers. After they rolled down the hill for several hours, their newly grown wool sported loud, tie-dye designs. One sheep's wool actually grew a plaid design! People stopped their cars to stare as they grazed on the hillside.

Jimmy set up a little market stand along the road by the farm, and business went through the roof. People came from miles around to buy the designer eggs, the rainbow-colored woolen mittens and sweaters, and the delicious flavored milks.

Oma got a brand-new souped-up wheelchair, complete with a lawnmower engine. "A guy in town rigged it up for me, Jimmy!" Oma shouted. "Now I can really move!" With her wheelchair shaking wildly, grass and debris spouted out the back, and she cut a path wherever she went. Oma kept busy by leading tours of the farm for children's field trips. She couldn't hear most of their questions, but she always entertained the children.

Oma spent the rest of her time knitting and tending to the garden behind the house. Though she wasn't very good at gardening, she somehow produced the most exotic flowers Jimmy's parents had ever seen. Giant corn and thick, round grapes grew in abundance, as well as a host of vegetables, all quite different than the grocery-store variety.

In short time Mrs. Dabble's injury healed, and together she and Mr. Dabble did their new daily chores of answering mail, dealing with the stock market, hiring more employees, and even charity work. They simply didn't understand how any of it worked, but they liked the results, and opted not to question Jimmy. The farm ran like a finely tuned engine, with a buzz of harmonious activity. Their money worries were gone. Mr. Dabble's pipe was once again filled with tobacco, the finest grade. And Mrs. Dabble's knickknack shelf

grew crowded with little figurines. Her new favorite was of a little boy lying in the grass, daydreaming.

Al did absolutely nothing. Guaranteed to live a long life, he ate like a hog and lay in the mud all day, humming little tunes. He gradually cultivated his voice to the degree that he could take on the classics. Jimmy's parents simply ignored the fact that they had a pig that sang like Pavarotti. One night, while his parents slept soundly, Jimmy gathered the animals in the new barn and recorded them singing Venetian love songs. Jimmy called the record "Puccini Goes to the Farm," and it was a big hit.

Jimmy never forgot Beebo. Occasionally he went into the dark woods to paint some trees or play in the stream. And even though Beebo had said good-bye, it couldn't mean forever. Jimmy knew that one day he'd see his friend again.